CROWNER & JUSTICE

CROWNER AND JUSTICE

Barrie Roberts

CHIVERS
THORNDIKE

This Large Print edition is published by BBC Audiobooks Ltd, Bath, England and by Thorndike Press, Waterville, Maine, USA.

Published in 2004 in the U.K. by arrangement with Headline Book Publishing.

Published in 2004 in the U.S. by arrangement with Allison & Busby Limited.

U.K. Hardcover   ISBN 0–7540–7732–2 (Chivers Large Print)
U.K. Softcover   ISBN 0–7540–7733–0 (Camden Large Print)
U.S. Softcover   ISBN 0–7862–6027–0 (General)

Copyright © 2002 by Barrie Roberts

The right of Barrie Roberts to be identified as the author of this work has been asserted by him in accordance with the Copyright, Designs and Patents Act 1988.

All rights reserved.

The text of this Large Print edition is unabridged.
Other aspects of the book may vary from the original edition.

Set in 16 pt. New Times Roman.

Printed in Great Britain on acid-free paper.

British Library Cataloguing in Publication Data available

Library of Congress Control Number: 2003111310

AUTHOR'S NOTE

The Metropolitan Borough of Belston does not exist. If it did, it would probably be one of the so-called 'Black Country Boroughs' that lie north-west of Birmingham; since it doesn't, it isn't! All characters, events and organisations in this story are completely fictitious, except the Employment Tribunals, which are unbelievable fact.

PROLOGUE

Nobody thinks about dying when they're eighteen. Sex and drugs and rock 'n' roll is more like it. Dying is not on the agenda. Life is your credit card and it's always someone else's bill that comes in stamped 'AIDS' or 'car crash' or 'murder'.

Sean McBride was eighteen so he wasn't thinking about dying. Sean was thinking about a girl with long slender legs and soft lips and bright eyes and . . . he took out a cigarette, lit it and slid a bit lower in his seat, stretched his legs and breathed the smoke in deeply, smiling the fatuous grin of the contented. He thought about the girl again, about a weekend with her at his mate's place in Yorkshire. They'd planned weekends before, but they'd never managed one. They weren't going to make it this time, either, but he never found that out. Sean McBride was eighteen and he'd just begun dying faster than he'd ever expected.

CHAPTER ONE

Have you noticed how all those fictional detectives—Rebus, Jack Reacher, even Miss Marple—hate coincidences? Apart from the late Endeavour Morse, who thought his life was beset by coincidences. Sherlock Holmes said that, 'Coincidence, Watson, is the willing handmaiden of a lazy mind'. Well, the real detectives hate coincidences, too. I've heard Detective Inspector John Parry of the Central Midlands CID remark more than once that, 'Coincidence stinks, boyo—like old fish'. Not as neat, perhaps, but it makes the point.

I never even noticed the coincidence in the first place. That was because I was too busy. My assistant, Alasdair, was on holiday; my articled clerk was sick; so there I was—stuck seeing clients.

Sometimes I dream about being the kind of solicitor who never sees a client in the office. You know—like some of the big blokes in Brum. Toddle into the office about mid-morning. Get an assistant who will read the mail to tell you if there's anything in it you ought to know. Make a few phone calls. Amble off to lunch for a few hours. Perhaps fetch up on the golf course. Meet a client there. Take a holdall full of drug money from him in the changing room. Launder it through your client account, and the next time you meet him will be on a beach in the Seychelles where you're both spending your ill-gotten gains.

There's a theory that you can get high just from handling banknotes from rich lawyers—either from the cocaine they use or the heroin their clients peddle. It's only a theory—nobody's ever found a way of taking money from a rich lawyer.

It doesn't work like that down at my end of the market. Tyrolls, Solicitors, of Jubilee Buildings, Belston, West Midlands, is not into mid-morning arrivals, long lunches, golfing, money laundering or holidays in the Seychelles. We're into early arrivals, late nights, missed lunches and short holidays if any. As to money laundering—well, once in a while we defend a drug-dealer. When we do, he applies for Legal Aid and gets it, while his profits are sprouting interest in clumps in some other solicitor's nominee account in the Cayman Islands, and when strangers at parties ask his solicitor if he defends criminals he tells them that he leaves that end of the market to other firms, he only deals with the commercial end where everybody's honest.

Crime, matrimonials, accident claims and all the bits and pieces that they call 'litigation' is our business. Most of it is conducted on Legal Aid, and there isn't a politician of any party who doesn't regard the Legal Aid fund as a legitimate target for reductions. So, as sole partner in Tyrolls, I support an assistant solicitor (who's found time for a holiday), an articled clerk (who's found time to be ill), a book-keeper, two secretaries and a receptionist. Not very well, as they often remind me.

The day it all started was a hot one in late summer. I had done my stint in two Magistrates' Courts that morning, missed lunch and now I had three people in front of me. Con Mulvaney, Jim Martin and Mohammed Afsar. Mulvaney, forties, broad built, wide-faced, fair, fresh-complexioned, thinning hair, nicotine-stained fingers, chainstore suit in lovat, trade union tie; Martin, thirties, slight, long, narrow, humorous face, ginger medium length hair, dark blazer and flannels, open-necked red shirt; Afsar, mid-twenties, lean, dark, thin moustache, good dark grey suit, white shirt, dark blue tie.

Mulvaney introduced himself and the others as they filed in and took chairs.

'It's Mr Thayne, is it?' he asked me. Despite the Irish name the accent was somewhere north of Belston.

I shook my head. 'My assistant, I'm afraid, has gone away and left you to me. I'm Chris Tyroll'.

'Nothing like going straight to the top', observed Martin.

'I don't know if Alasdair Thayne knew what your problem is', I said, 'but I'm starting fresh, so you'll have to tell me'.

Mulvaney nodded. 'That's alright', he said. 'We phoned Mr Thayne because a friend recommended him, but we haven't told him anything about it'.

I looked at the three of them and tried to guess at a mutual interest. 'Well, you don't look as if the problem's a marital one, and nobody's injured, so it's not an accident claim. What sort of case are we talking about?'

'An employment tribunal', said Mulvaney, and I groaned inwardly. When the Labour Party invented Legal Aid back in the forties, they thought they'd do it in three stages, so as not to swamp the profession with a tidal wave of new work. First they brought in Legal Aid in the criminal courts; next came Legal Aid in the civil courts. The third stage was intended to be Legal Aid in the administrative tribunals, employment, welfare, health and so on. The only problem was that after the first two parts were implemented, they realised that it was costing several fortunes, so they did what politicians always do when the money frightens them—they stopped short. So, you can't get Legal Aid for representation in a tribunal. That means you end up acting for people who've lost their jobs and can't pay the bill afterwards.

'You may not be aware', I said, 'that Legal Aid is not available in the Employment Tribunals'.

Mulvaney nodded. 'I know', he confirmed. 'You see, the thing is, we were going to do it ourselves; I've been a Shop Steward for years. I've seen people through tribunals and disciplinary hearings, but the word is that the firm's taking this very seriously and putting a battery of lawyers on it, so the boys thought we needed a lawyer'.

'I don't charge as much as some of the firms around here', I said, 'but it'll still cost a lot—more according to how long it runs. Is it a complicated case? Which of you has applied to the Tribunal?'

'All of us', said Martin, and grinned. 'We was all sacked at once'.

'For the same reason?' I asked.

'Not quite', said Mulvaney. 'I was sacked for calling a strike, Jim was sacked for agreeing with me, and Mohammed was sacked for walking off the job, which was what the strike was about'.

A vague recollection stirred, a memory of headlines and TV news bulletins earlier in the summer.

'You worked at BDS?' I said. 'You're the people who threatened the defence of Britain, according to the *Daily Telegraph*? Is that right?'

'That's right', said Mulvaney. 'Traitors, according to the *Sun*', smiled Martin.

More memories stirred. BDS—British Defence Systems—had a big plant on the

Belston ring road and another in Coventry. They used to have three more up north, but Mrs Thatcher saw to them. They'd been working to produce a new missile, the Retaliator. I'd seen it demonstrated on TV—a sleek, sea-green device that could be launched on land or sea or in the air and would hunt its target using the camera in its nose and the satellite guidance systems. It was going to be lighter and faster and pack more clout than any known missile; its guidance systems would be the most sensitive. Once it locked onto a target it could not be shaken off and was almost impossible to shoot down. Anyway, that's what BDS said. Once our forces had it, we'd be quickest on the draw in any confrontation. Then they'd make a fortune selling it all over the world until someone who'd bought it sold it to someone who didn't like us and our blokes would get killed by a British-made Retaliator. Then BDS would get a fat contract to make something even better, or perhaps I'm just being cynical.

Earlier in the summer there'd been a sudden strike at BDS's Belston works. The management said it was unjustifiable. The Union said it was not official, but it spread to the Coventry plant. Then, just as suddenly as it began, it ended. The Retaliator was undergoing trials and all was well with the world. Apart from my three clients.

'So, BDS want to make an example of you.

The right-wing press will be cheering them on, and you want me to stop them?'

'If you would, like', said Martin.

'I charge extra for miracles', I said. 'Tell me, why won't your Union help you?'

Mulvaney and Martin laughed. Mohammed smiled wryly.

'Because they're in it', said Mulvaney. 'They helped BDS to stop the strike. They're thick as thieves. That's why the boys on the shop-floor said we were to get a lawyer and they'll pay'.

'Who will?' I asked.

'The lads. At BDS. They want to see us win, so they're holding collections each payday. We'll find the money'.

'And you were sacked for the reasons you said?'

'Well, there was one other thing', said Martin. 'That's against all three of us. They say we attacked the Works Manager'.

I groaned silently again and reached for a notepad. 'You'd better tell me about it', I said. 'Who's first?'

CHAPTER TWO

It took an hour to get even the outline of their story noted, but I'd got other clients, so I made the three trade unionists another appointment and moved on. My next client was John

Samson, who I'd never seen before.

He turned out to be a stocky bloke in his late thirties, with a local accent. He was one of three partners in a small business that made harness fittings. Walsall, just up the road, is the world centre of fine leather harness. The old Hollywood cowboy stars used to have their saddles and gunbelts made in Walsall; now it's Arab millionaires. Samson's firm turned out the small metal fittings that go with harness.

That sounded a deal less controversial than making the world's nastiest weaponry, but I wondered what brought him to me.

'It's my daughter', he said. 'She wanted a pony'.

Everybody's daughter wants a pony at some time or another and it isn't illegal, though a lot of fathers wish it was. It turned out that Samson's daughter and the daughter of one of his partners at work both wanted ponies. Most fathers can't afford ponies for their daughters, so their daughters grow up a bit and transfer their frustrated equine desires to something else ungainly and toothy with long hair, bulging eyes and an uncertain temper and call it a boyfriend.

Unluckily for Samson and his mate they could afford ponies, so they asked around their contacts in the trade and eventually they were offered two decent animals at a bargain price. They snatched at the bargain quickly. Too quickly, in fact, because they hadn't got anywhere to keep two ponies.

Both of them live in Kerren Wood, a village just outside Belston and, being a village, it has fields round it. One of those fields was never used, so they asked about to see if anyone knew who owned it. Nobody seemed to know, so they popped their daughters' mounts in there and left them grazing happily. To be fair, they didn't just take over somebody else's field; they left a note at the local police station so that if someone came enquiring about strange ponies on his patch the police could let him know who owned the animals and that they wanted to rent his field.

All very reasonable, and it should have worked. However, their daughters went along to the field one Sunday tea-time and there the ponies were—gone. A quick visit to the police station revealed that the owner of the field had turned up, told the police that he wasn't interesting in letting his field and that he was seizing the ponies, which he did.

'Do you know who he was?' I asked.

'Oh, yes', said Samson. 'He left his particulars with the police. He's a businessman in Brum'.

'So, why do you need a lawyer?'

'Well, can he do that? Can he just take our ponies, just like that?'

'Probably', I said. 'After all, it was his field and you put your ponies in it without his permission. How long had they been there?'

'About six weeks'.

'So, you owe him for about six weeks grazing, if nothing else, which, I suspect, gives him the right to seize your animals until his bill is paid. Have you had a bill from him?'

'No'.

'Right, well, I can write to him on your behalf, asking for a bill for what's due and repeating your offer to rent his field. Then we'll see if he'll be reasonable'.

'He hasn't been very bloody reasonable so far', complained Samson.

'Don't worry', I said. 'I'm sure we can sort this out quickly and amicably and get your daughter's pony back'.

I was wrong about that, but it put me in a better frame of mind to see my next client, Mrs McBride.

Mrs McBride was very large, red-haired, and very Irish.

Despite the sweltering afternoon she was wearing a tweed cape, and she clutched a bulging cardboard folder to her ample chest. Plonking herself into a chair opposite me, she flipped the folder open, then scrabbled in her handbag for a packet of cigarettes. Once she had one in her mouth I lit it for her.

'My name's Chris Tyroll', I said. 'What can I do for you, Mrs McBride?'

She looked up, staring intensely into my face.

'You can get me justice!' she declared in a

strong Irish accent

'I'll try', I said. 'What's the problem?'

'My son was murdered', she announced, 'that's the problem'.

CHAPTER THREE

There's something about spells of hot weather that brings the nutters flooding into solicitors' offices. You know—the ones who are heirs to the Czar's gold in the vaults of the Bank of England, the ones who are the rightful Queens of England, the ones who own Edinburgh Castle. They usually sit at home in their flats and their bedsitters, going through their files of news cuttings and their carrier bags full of papers and in cold weather they stay by the fire, but hot weather makes them restless and they decide to do something about their delusory claims. Then there's the ones who, as soon as the sun turns hot in the sky, start having arguments with their neighbours that turn into bitter disputes over fences and kids and tree branches and pigeon coops. I've grown well used to them and expect them every time there's a heatwave, so I gritted my teeth and reached for my notebook.

While I listened to Mrs McBride's story the rest of the office shut down around me. At last I thought I understood her argument. I was tired and hot. My shirt was sticking to me and my tie was strangling me.

I gave a promise to look into the matter for her, showed her out and locked the door behind her. It was too hot to walk home up the hill to Whiteway Village, so I called a cab.

I was dropped off outside my garden gate and ambled around the side of the house. I guessed that Sheila would be on the patio at the back and, as I rounded the side of the house, I could hear her strumming a guitar and singing:

'Then the miller he took all her guineas ten,
Hey down, bow down.
Then the miller he took all her guineas ten.
And he pushed the fair maid in again,
Singing I'll be true to my true love.
If my love will be true to me.
Then the Crowner he came and the justice too,
Hey down, bow down,
Then the Crowner he came and the Justice too
With a hue and cry and hullabaloo,
Singing I'll be true to my true love
If my love will be true to me'.

As I turned the corner onto the patio, Sheila was revealed, sprawled in a garden chair, wearing skimpy white shorts and top and clutching a guitar. Sheila is Dr Sheila

McKenna, teacher of Social History at the University of Adelaide. About a year earlier she had come to Britain to visit her sole surviving relative, her grandfather. He had been a client of mine and was murdered on the very day that Sheila landed in England. Sorting that mess out cost both of us a lot of danger and nervous tension, in the course of which she decided she'd like to marry me, and then she disappeared back to Australia.

This year she was back on a year's sabbatical leave from her department so she could research and write a book on the convicts transported to Oz. Even that didn't keep her out of trouble. Her researches upset someone who responded with firebombs and booby traps. Altogether an interesting lady to be around—if she'd ever stop bouncing back and forth to Australia.

She looked up as I appeared.

'Bushed?' she asked.

'Cream-crackered', I agreed.

'Cream-crackered?' she queried.

'Knackered', I said. 'Totally', I added, falling onto a bench. 'What I need is a long, cool drink'.

She reached for a bottle on the table at her side and poured me a tall glass of something pale yellow.

'White wine', she said, passing it across, it's not bad'.

'Not so', I said, when I'd taken half of it at a

swallow and was beginning to come back to life. 'That is not any kind of wine. That is Britain's greatest gift to the world of drink—still perry'.

'I thought perry was fizzy, sweet stuff that dirty old men give to teenage girls 'cos they reckon they won't get spliffed on it', she said, frowning.

'So it is', I said, 'though the nation that invented alcoholic lemonade can hardly criticise. This, on the other hand, is a still perry from Herefordshire, than which there is no more ideal summer drink'.

'Well, cheers then', she said, and poured herself another large one.

'Tell me', I said, 'why were you intoning that daft old song? Where'd you get it from?'

'It's not a daft old song and I found it on one of your late mother's records'.

I nodded. 'My late mother', I said, 'used to get paid small sums of money for singing ancient quaintnesses like that to small groups of aficionados in draughty upper rooms over pubs many years ago. She also used to sing them to me as lullabies'.

'What—that one?' Sheila exclaimed.

'Even that one—"The Berkshire Tragedy", to give it a proper name'.

She laughed. 'So there's these two sisters after the same bloke, and one tries to bribe the other to give him up, and when she won't her sister pushes her in the river, and she floats down the river till a miller fishes her out with a pole and hook and she offers him ten guineas to take her home and ...'

'... the miller takes the money and pushes her back in the river and she drowns', I continued the story.

'Then the Crowner he comes—what's a Crowner?' she asked.

'A Coroner', I said. 'A tax officer charged under the medieval Statute of Coronary with investigating mysterious deaths'.

'A tax officer?'

'Yup. The view was taken that murders and mysterious deaths were usually about money, so a Coroner's duty was to investigate and see if there was any money involved that the King could take in tax or fines'.

'And your mum used to sing you to sleep with that song?'

'Not just me, but audiences all over the country. Sometimes I think that song is the principal reason why the Folk Revival went back to sleep'.

Sheila shook her head. 'No wonder you grew up warped', she said, and picked up her guitar again.

'Don't', I said, 'sing songs about Coroners, please. I have had an Irish lady banging on at me for more than hour about how the Belston Coroner has covered up her son's murder as suicide. I am not into Coroners tonight'.

'Sounds interesting', she said. 'Tell me

about it'.

I took another long draught of perry. 'I will tell you about it on one condition—that while I'm showering you will prepare an enormous meal of something cold and sustaining accompanied by two more bottles of chilled perry'.

To my surprise she agreed without a murmur.

An hour later the heat had gone off the day and my mind was at least slightly less tangled. Sheila and I sat on the patio over the remains of a large cold repast, breaking the second bottle of perry and watching the sun sinking beyond the garden. I was beginning to feel human again.

'Right', she announced. 'Time to tell'.

Telling a story to another person always helps to put things in the right order in your head. Sometimes it helps you to see what's important and what isn't.

I filled my glass, took a sip and began.

'Mrs McBride is a middle-aged Irish lady who lives on the Orchard estate. She works part-time, as a cleaner for a couple of different customers and she has a school-age daughter, about nine. She did have an eighteen-year-old son called Sean'.

'The one who was murdered?' Sheila interrupted.

'The one who his mother thinks was murdered', I corrected.

'What happened to him, then?'

'On a Friday evening in May, Sean was at home. He had said that he was going on a short holiday the next morning, and Mrs M had been washing and ironing for him. So far as she knew, he wasn't going out that night because he had to be up early in the morning to travel'.

'What did he do for a living?'

'Don't interrupt or I'll get it all wrong! He had been an engineering apprentice at BDS, but they're mean buggers and they usually let a lot of apprentices go once they start expecting a full wage, so he was working as a mechanic at a mate's garage'.

I drank again before continuing.

'On that Friday evening, a friend of his came to the back door of the house, and he and Sean had a chat'.

'What about?'

'I don't know. His mother didn't hear, but after a bit he came and said that he was going out for a while. His mum told him not to be too late because of his early start. That was the last time she saw him alive. He went off with his mate and she never saw him again'.

'So, where did he go? His mate must know'.

'His mate says that it never happened, that he never called at the house that night and he never saw Sean that evening. That's what he told the Coroner, apparently'.

'But his mother knew who the caller was,

surely?'

'Ah well, not quite. Sean had answered the door, talked to someone at the door and then told his mum that he was just going out for a while with Charlie. Mum never actually saw Charlie. It appears that, when this came out in front of the Coroner, he decided that Mrs M was mistaken and that the caller had been someone else'.

'Could have been', Sheila commented.

'So it could, but Mrs M is absolutely certain that it was Charlie'.

'Do you believe her?'

'I believe that she believes it was Charlie. I don't know what else I believe. Can I go on?'

'Fire away'.

'Sean never came home that night. Mrs M worried—not too much because he was eighteen, after all, and he was a big lad who could usually take care of himself, but when the weekend had passed, she rang the police. They, of course, didn't want to know, as they almost never want to know about missing teenagers. Then Charlie turned up, asking if Sean was back from his weekend trip'.

'So he thought Sean had gone away?'

'Apparently. Mrs M told him she hadn't seen Sean since Friday night and asked him where Sean was. He said he didn't know'.

'Did he admit that he'd gone off with Sean on Friday night?'

'He didn't admit it, but Mrs M says he didn't

deny it, either'.

'That's pretty peculiar, isn't it?'

'Yes, it is. Mrs M spent Monday asking anyone she thought might have seen Sean if they knew anything about him, but no one had seen him all weekend. Then, on Tuesday morning, the police arrived on her doorstep. He'd been found dead'.

'Where and how?'

'He had a car that he kept in a lock-up garage, a few streets away from his home. Mrs M had been there, but it was all locked up and she hadn't got a key'.

'So how was he found?'

'Charlie found him'.

'Charlie?!'

'The very same. It seems that Charlie thought that Sean might be in his garage . . .'

'Why?'

'Good question. I don't know. Charlie just had this thought out of the blue, so he went along on Tuesday morning only to find that the place was all locked up'.

'Who had a key?'

'Only Sean it seems, but if he was murdered, someone else must have had. Charlie checked the only door and it was locked. So he climbed up on the roof, because he knew there was a loose area in the roofing and he thought he could get in'.

'Why did he want to get in, if the place was locked? Why didn't he think that Sean couldn't be in there, like Mrs M?'

'Another good question. Anyway, whatever the reason, he got up on the roof and looked in through the loose area. He could see the front of the car and Sean's foot in the passenger seat area, so he scrambled down again and called the police. They forced the door and found Sean dead in the rear seat of his car'.

'What did he die of?'

'Carbon monoxide poisoning—exhaust fumes'.

'You mean a hosepipe in the exhaust job?'

'No. That's part of the problem. He died because the engine had run in the garage and the garage was largely airtight'.

'Which he must have known?'

'Right'.

'And the door was locked?'

'Right'.

'So he sat in his car, with the engine running, in a locked garage to which only he had a key, and which he must have known was airtight. Right?'

'Right'.

'Sounds like suicide to me, Chris'.

'That's what the Coroner thought. That's what the death certificate says. Mrs M disagrees'.

Sheila mused a while over her drink.

'So he was about to go off for a weekend', she said at last. 'With a girl—a bloke—was he straight or gay?'

'Straight, so far as his mother knew'.

'Everybody's straight so far as their mother knows. Did he have a current girlfriend?'

'Yes'.

'You never said so'.

'You never asked and anyway, she didn't give evidence at the Inquest'.

'What might she have said?'

'We don't know—she never said it'.

'Who was she?'

'Now there you're on an interesting trail. She was a fifteen-year-old schoolgirl at the Abbey Gate School'.

'That's a bit posh, isn't it?'

'It certainly is—children of thirty-second degree Masons and minor royalty only'.

'And which is her dad?'

'Well, he might be in the first group. He's a lawyer, a top commercial bloke, always whizzing off to see clients in Singapore and Miami and San Francisco'.

'So he'd have been pretty upset at his lovely daughter wasting herself on a garage bloke?'

'I imagine so, if he knew'.

'Did he know?'

'I don't know'.

She glared at me. 'It strikes me, Chris Tyroll, that there's a lot about this case you don't know. Hasn't anyone interviewed the girl?'

'No. The Coroner's Officer was most

anxious that that shouldn't happen'.

'What's a Coroner's Officer?'

'A policeman—usually a Sergeant—assigned to assist a Coroner'.

'And why didn't he interview the girl?'

'Mrs McBride tells me that she asked him to. She thought the girl might shed some light on Sean's death, but the Sergeant was adamant. He was more than that, in fact. She says that, when she tried to push it with him, he banged his fist on the desk and kept shouting at her, telling her that Sylvia Wellington was a schoolgirl from a nice family who wouldn't want her mixed up in this affair and that he wasn't going to get her mixed up in this affair. He wasn't *going* to interview her or involve her in any way, and Mrs M could face up to the fact that her boy's death was accident or suicide, whichever the Coroner decided'.

'That sounds pretty hard. Do you know this Coroner's Officer bloke? Is he usually like that?'

I shook my head. 'Coroner's Officers are usually chosen because they can be relied on to do their job without upsetting the relatives of the deceased. That's the sort of man Sergeant Wilson is'.

'So what do you make of Mrs M's tale about him?'

'Mrs McBride is a highly emotional Irish lady, whose son has died. She gets angry and upset very easily and she shouts at people. She did at me a few times and I'm supposed to be on her side. Maybe she did that at Sergeant Wilson and he lost his rag at her. But I still can't see him telling her that he wouldn't involve the girl'.

'So you don't believe her?'

'I find that part hard to believe. As to the rest, well, the garage door was locked and only Sean had a key'.

'Might still have been an accident', Sheila said. 'Surely there's got to be some indication of a reason for a Coroner to find suicide?'

'Right. He said that the boy had been having headaches and that he was worried about a driving prosecution and that, as teenagers do, he magnified it all out of proportion and committed suicide'.

'Had he been having headaches? Was he being prosecuted?'

'Mrs M says that she never knew he was being prosecuted, but the Coroner's Officer picked it up. Sean was awaiting trial for driving with excess alcohol. As to headaches, Mrs M insists that Sean was robustly healthy and had never complained of a headache in his life'.

'So that's not true?'

'Apparently not, but it is true that the Coroner gave that as his reason for finding suicide. She showed me the press report of the Inquest'.

'So, then, Sherlock, what do you make of it all?'

'I'm damned if I know, Watson!'
'Sherlock never said that!'
'I'll bet he did. It's just that Watson never let on'.

CHAPTER FOUR

It was less hectic the next day. I had no court appearances, so I could sit in the office and try to tidy up my notes from the previous afternoon.

I started with what I thought was the easy one—Samson's daughter's pony. A polite letter to the bloke who'd seized the ponies', saying that I was instructed by the ponies owners, that they were very sorry that they'd trespassed on his field, but they had nowhere to graze their animals and hadn't been able to find out who owned the field; they would gladly pay reasonable fees for the weeks of grazing that they'd had and would he please consider letting them rent the field in the long term. Very persuasive, I thought. No reasonable bloke could refuse an offer to make money out of a field that he wasn't using, surely.

Next it was the BDS strike. It seemed to have started with Mohammed Afsar, so I started trying to put my notes in the form of a proof of evidence.

'MOHAMMED AFSAR states that:

I am 26 years old and single. I live with my parents at 37 Hospital Terrace, Belston, West Midlands.

I am unemployed at present, but was recently working for BDS at Belston as a Computer Programmer. I hold a degree in Computer Studies from the University of Bradford and, after leaving university, was employed for some years by the Communications Corporation at Swindon.

I started work at BDS about two and a half years ago. I cannot describe my work in detail, as it is covered by the Official Secrets Act, but in general I was concerned with the software which controls the launching and guidance of the Retaliator missile.

I worked in the Computer Department under a Mr Swan. In the early stages of my work there I found it very interesting. Incidents during the Gulf War and in Bosnia had made it necessary to refine guidance systems so that there was virtually no chance of an error in targeting. At first the management of BDS was always hurrying our department up, so that Retaliator could be tried out on test ranges.

In the early part of this year we found that things were changing. There seemed to be difficulties with the mechanical and electronic development of Retaliator and our work became less urgent. In fact, things turned right around. We were developing software which we believed would do the jobs required, but the necessary circuitry or mechanisms had not been developed so that we were unable to try out our programs in practice. It was very frustrating.

At the same time, it seemed that BDS were cost-cutting. All sorts of staff were let go, in almost all departments, to the extent that there were frequently not enough personnel to man some of the production lines. There was a notice at the main gate, advertising casual vacancies to be filled. As each shift clocked on, the shift foreman would be told to check if they had the men that they needed and, if not, to notify vacancies to the main gate. There was usually a queue there of men from the Jobcentre who knew that there was always a chance of getting a shift's work at BDS, and the security men at the gate would let in as many as were needed and send them to the departments that were short.

When I first joined BDS I became a member of the Union, the Munitions Industry Union. It has a reputation as a 'company union' because it is the one that the Government prefers to operate in defence factories, but my father is a great believer in trade unions and told me that I must join. The MIU was, in fact, the only trade union that BDS would recognise on its premises.

Although I thought that MIU was a

company union, I was pleasantly surprised by its activities at BDS. The Shop Stewards were very keen and the Chairman of the Shop Stewards, Mr Mulvaney, was very aware of what was going on all over the plant.

I know that Mr Mulvaney and the Shop Stewards were extremely unhappy about the practice of undermanning. They said that an awful lot of time was wasted in training unskilled casual labour and a lot of product was wasted in the process. They kept arguing with the management that the whole system needed to be completely re-organised and enough labour hired to do all the work properly. The management kept saying that times were difficult and that they hadn't got the funds to hire at will. They kept telling us that once Retaliator was up and running and the government orders were in, there would money in plenty and everything could be put right.

The whole of the workforce was affected by the undermanning, and everyone was getting increasingly fed up with it. Several times, at Union meetings, it was suggested that we strike if there was no agreement by the management to adopt a proper manning policy. Mr Mulvaney always argued against striking.

I did not believe that the undermanning would affect the Computer Department, as there was no way that they could make us use unskilled labour. In the end, however, it affected us the other way round. Because we could not get on with our work on the Retaliator software, the management started using staff from our department to carry out all sorts of computer work in other departments. On a number of occasions I was asked to help out in the Accounts, Progress and Stores Departments.

The work we were asked to do instead of our own work was routine keyboarding of information into the firms management programs, work that could be done by anyone who can read and press keys. I am not a snob, but that is not the work that I trained for and took my degree for, nor is it the job that I was contracted for with BDS. I would not have minded assisting in an emergency, but these were not emergencies, they were situations created by BDS' persistent undermanning.

Things came to a head on the morning of Friday 15th May. Mr Swan came to me and asked if I was busy. He knew that I was not, that our whole department was just marking time, waiting until our software could be tested.

I told him that I was just trying to refine the landscape recognition programs, but he knew we'd done that over and over again and that we couldn't make any progress without testing.

He said that they needed help in Accounts. I said that I had had enough of being used as supernumerary labour in the Accounts office and that it wasn't what I had been employed to do. My Contract of Employment engaged me as a Computer Programmer and set out my duties in the Computer Department; it didn't say that I had to work as an Accounts Clerk as well.

Mr Swan said that he sympathised with me, but that Mr Greene in Accounts said that he had permission to borrow someone from our department. I said that I didn't care, that I would not go.

Mr Swan said that he'd have to tell Mr Greene that I had refused. I said that he could go ahead and tell him, that I was not doing work other than my own duties.

Mr Swan phoned Mr Greene and told him what I had said. A few minutes later the phone rang and it was Mr Bailey, the Managing Director. He spoke to Mr Swan briefly, then Mr Swan put me on the phone.

Bailey said to me:

'I'm told that you refuse to help out in Accounts?'

I said:

'I've told Mr Swan that I was employed as a Computer Programmer, not an Accounts Clerk. I do not wish to work in Accounts'.

Bailey said:

'And suppose I order you to go to the Accounts Department?'

I said:

'I am very sorry, Mr Bailey, but I am employed as a Computer Programmer and I will not go to the Accounts Department or any other department again'.

He said:

'Listen, young man. You were employed to work for BDS and to do what your superiors tell you. As far as I'm concerned, if you refuse to do as you're told, you're refusing a legitimate command of your employer and you can be sacked on the spot. Do you understand me?'

I said:

'I understand you perfectly, Mr Bailey, but what you are telling me to do is not a part of my work and is not a legitimate command. I have to tell you that I will not do it'.

He said:

'Right! I warned you and you wouldn't listen. You can get off the premises. I don't want to see you again. Any pay that's due to you will be sent on. Just get out!'

He put the phone down and I told Mr Swan what had been said.

He looked uncomfortable and he said, 'I'm afraid that there's nothing I can do, Mohammed. You know what the Boss is like when he's got one on him. If he says you've got to go, that's it. Let it go a few days and I'll see if he'll have you back once he's calmed down'.

I cleared my desk and I went home. I told my father what had happened and he phoned

Mr Bailey. He told me afterwards that Mr Bailey only said that I had refused to do what I was told and that he wasn't interested in employing people who only did what they wanted to. My father then told me to talk to the Union.

I phoned Mr Mulvaney at the factory and he said to come and see him at home that night.

I went to see him and told him what had happened. He was very sympathetic and said that it was not a legitimate order to make me work in the Accounts Department. He said that it all came out of the firm's undermanning and that he was sick and tired of trying to make them see sense. After he thought about it a bit, he said that he would get on to the National Secretary of the Union and see if he could think of something. Mr Mulvaney rang me at home on the Saturday and said that he was going down to London on Monday to see Mr Capstick, the National Secretary. He asked if I would like to come with him and I agreed to go . . .'

I had got that far with Mohammed's evidence when there was a tap at my door and Jayne, my secretary looked in.

'Tracy's here', she said. 'Tracy Walton. She wondered if she could have a word. Said it was urgent'.

I sighed and put down my dictation mike.

'Go on', I said. 'Show her in'.

CHAPTER FIVE

Jayne was back in a moment, leading a large woman in her fifties, with bleached blonde hair and a face whose natural expression seemed to be one of slight wariness. When she was seated I offered her a cigarette.

'How are you, Tracy?' I said. 'Your husband's not in trouble again, is he?'

She shook her head. 'Oh, no, Mr Tyroll', she said. 'Never again. He's alright now. He's working for the Council'.

In the spring I had succeeded in overturning a long ago conviction which freed Tracy's husband from prison. It hadn't been much fun, and I was glad to hear she didn't need the same service again.

'It's about Kathleen', she said, 'Kathleen McBride'.

'You know her?' I asked.

'She lives on our street. It was me as sent her to you, Mr Tyroll. She was that desperate to get something done about poor Sean and I told how you'd got my Alan out of jail'.

'So you knew Sean?'

'That's right', she nodded. 'He'd wouldn't have done that you know, Mr Tyroll. He was a good-natured, cheerful sort of lad'.

'So, what was it you wanted to talk about, Tracy?'

'Kath come to see me after she'd been here yesterday', she said. 'She give me a right going over. Said she day think you believed her'.

'About what?'

'About any of it. She said you kept asking how this could happen and how that could happen, how the door was locked and he had the only key and all that'.

'It's my job to test what people tell me, Tracy. If it ends up in a court, other people will test it hard, so it's my job to test it first and see if it stands up'.

'And did you believe her?' she asked bluntly.

'It isn't up to me to believe or disbelieve her. The rules say that I've got to take what she tells me and do the best I can with it unless I actually know something's not true. I don't know any of it's not true, Tracy, but there are bits I find hard to believe—like the door. If nobody else had a key to Sean's garage, then no one else got in there to kill him. And the Coroner's Officer, I find that hard to believe'.

'What, about him shouting at her?'

'Yes. He's just not like that, Tracy'.

She snorted. 'He mightn't be like that with you, Mr Tyroll, but he was bloody horrible to poor Kath'.

'Really?' I said.

'He shouted at her, Mr Tyroll. He thumped on his desk. He was real nasty to her'.

'You were there, then?'

'Oh yes. I went along with her'.

'Do you remember what started him off?'

'He said that it was all very sad, but it looked like an open and shut case of suicide. Kath said as she couldn't believe that and he asked her why anyone would want to kill Sean. She said that she reckoned it was something to do with Sylvia Wellington and someone ought to talk to her. That's when he went off'.

'When Sylvia Wellington was mentioned?'

'That's right. He said as Sylvia Wellington was only a schoolgirl and her father was an important man and nobody would thank Kath for getting Wellington's daughter mixed up in a suicide inquest'.

'What did she say?'

'She said as Sean had been seeing Sylvia for quite a while and if anyone knew anything about him, she ought to'.

'Perfectly reasonable, but that's what started the Sergeant off?'

'That's right. He went really wild at Kath. He said he wasn't going to go bothering the girl, that she'd be upset enough already and he wasn't dragging her into the Inquest. Kath said as it was his duty and he shouted at her that nobody was going to tell him his duty, it was a plain case of suicide and Kath should accept it. He was so angry I knew we warn't going to get nowhere with him, so I took Kath's arm and I said, "Come on, love, we ay going to get nowhere with this man", and we went'.

No one was more believable than Tracy

Walton. I was kicking myself for falling for racial stereotyping. An upset Irishwoman with tears in her eyes tells me something peculiar and I couldn't believe it, but Tracy, sitting in front of me all solid and Black Country, was completely believable. Something about the Wellington girl really had freaked out the Coroner's Officer. Was it just the power and influence of her father? A thought occurred to me.

'Were you at the Inquest?' I asked.

'That's right', she said. 'I went along with Kath'.

'Do you remember what was said?'

She looked up at the ceiling. 'Let's see', she said. 'There was Charlie Nesbit, he give evidence first. He said about how he and Sean was mates for years and how Sean had been missing all weekend and Kath had asked him if he knew where he was. He said he'd rung Kath to see if Sean was back and when she said he was still gone he'd thought he might be in his garage'.

'Did he say why he thought that?'

She shook her head. 'No. He just said he thought he'd have a look, so he went there and it was locked up, but he got on the roof, where he could see in'.

'Did he say why he thought that Sean would be in there if it was all locked up?'

'He said as he thought Sean might be locked in there, he thought he might have had an accident or something, so he got on the roof. When he looked and saw Sean he called out to him, but there wasn't any answer so he thought he'd better call the police'.

'Not an ambulance? He thought his mate had had an accident but he called the police, not an ambulance?'

'That's all he said, Mr Tyroll, as he thought he'd better call the police'.

'And nobody questioned him?'

'Not about that, no. He said he went to a phone box and called them'.

'Did anyone question him about anything?'

'Yes. When the Coroner said that Kath could ask questions, she asked him if he hadn't called at her house on the Friday night and gone off with Sean'.

'And what did he say?'

'He said he didn't, it must have been someone else'.

'Who else gave evidence?'

'There was a copper, a uniform, I don't remember his name. He said as they'd had a phone call from a phone box saying as someone had been found dead in a garage and he and another copper went to see what it was about. They went to the phone box on the corner of Wednesfield Road and Charlie Nesbit was there. He told them about how Sean had been missing all weekend and how he thought he might be in his garage, so he'd gone there and looked in through a hole in the roof and seen Sean's foot in the front of his car. He took them round to the garage and showed them that it was locked. Then he showed them how to get on the roof and the copper climbed up and saw what Charlie had seen, so they forced the door open. When they got inside, Sean's car was parked with the back to the door. The passenger's door was open wide and the passenger seat had been taken out and put on the floor. Sean was lying in the back seat, slumped down with his right knee up behind the driver's seat and his left leg where the passenger seat is usually'.

'And he was dead?'

'That's right, Mr Tyroll. The copper said as he could see that Sean was dead, but he called an ambulance. Kath asked him if Sean had any marks on him, like, but he said he never saw any. Then there was a doctor, who did the thingy, the post mortem'.

'That would have been Dr Macintyre, yes?'

'That's it. An old Scotch fellow with gingery hair. Looked like he liked a drop'.

I smiled to myself at the description of my old friend Mac. 'What had he got to say?' I asked.

'Oh, he said as he'd done the post mortem, as Sean was a healthy young man. He said there was no injuries on him and that he thought he'd died of inhaling whaterdeye-callit—carbon dioxide?'

'Carbon monoxide?'

'That's right. The Coroner asked him if he thought it was suicide and he said it warn't his place to say, as he was there to say how Sean died and that was by breathing in that carbon stuff, but wasn't going to say as it was suicide or an accident or something else. Then Kath asked him what he thought and he said much the same, that it was up to the police to investigate all the circumstances and the Coroner to decide what had happened. She asked if there was any sign of Sean being ill and he said as he never found none, and that was him finished'.

'Who was next?'

'Kath was next. She said about how Sean had been getting ready to go away for the weekend and she had been ironing his stuff for him on the Friday night, and she said how Charlie had come to the door and Sean had gone away with him. The Coroner questioned her a lot about that and then he said, "So, you never actually saw Mr Nesbit at your door. You only thought as it was him, and it might well have been someone else". She said as she was sure it was Charlie, but the Coroner wasn't having it. Then she said about how she'd looked for Sean and asked Charlie and his other friends about him, but no one had seen him and she said that the police had come and told her he'd been found and she'd had to go and identify his body. That made her really upset and the Coroner excused her'.

'Did the Coroner ask Kath anything about Sean's health?'

'Well, she said as he was alright, that there wasn't anything wrong with him'.

'She didn't say anything about headaches?'

'No. That was the Sergeant, the one who shouted at us. He was the last witness. He said as he'd talked to some of Sean's friends and they said as he had headaches. He was the one that said Sean was being taken to Court over a breathalyser. He said it was in the records'.

'So there was no medical evidence about Sean's headaches?'

She shook her head. 'No, Mr Tyroll. Only that Sergeant said about headaches'.

I reached for the file and pulled out some of the photocopies that Kath McBride had left with me the day before. One quoted the Coroner's summing-up:

'We have heard evidence that this young man was worried about his headaches, and that he was concerned about a prosecution for drink-driving. It is always difficult to fathom the mind of another person and particularly so with a teenager. I think it is fairly evident that, oppressed by matters which might not really have been of much concern, he took too black a view of his situation and, in a brief fit of depression, ended his own life'.

I read it over to Tracy. 'And that was it?' I asked.

'That's right', she said. 'That was what he

said'.

She stood up. 'I just wanted you to know as Kath was right about that Sergeant. He was horrible to her, Mr Tyroll'.

'Thanks', I said. 'Tell Kath that I'm asking the Coroner's Office for a copy of the notes of evidence and I'll be in touch with her'.

Tracy stood, thoughtfully, in the doorway, then turned back towards me.

'Has Kath told you about the song?' she asked.

'Song?' I said.

She nodded slowly. 'She was real upset last night, 'cos she thought as you didn't believe her, and we had a drink or two together and she said something she's never said before. She said someone keeps ringing her up and playing a song to her on the phone'.

'What song?' I asked, still feeling completely bewildered.

She shook her head. 'She did say, but it was some Irish song I day know. She says it's been happening ever since the Inquest, but she never mentioned it to you 'cos she thought you'd think she was wrong in the head'.

'Let me get this right', I said. 'Since Sean's Inquest, someone has been phoning Kath and playing a song to her?'

'That's right'.

'Always the same song?'

'That's right'.

'And they don't say anything?'

'That's right. She said as they just play the song—not all of it—then hang up'.

I stared at her for a moment. 'You tell Kath', I said at last, 'to keep a cassette recorder by the phone and bring me a tape of one of those calls'.

'She's got it on tape, Mr Tyroll, already'.

'Then tell her to bring the tape in tomorrow afternoon. I want to hear this song'.

'Righto, Mr Tyroll. I'll do that', and off she went.

I tried to settle down and dictate the remainder of Mohammed's proof of evidence and carry on with the general task of the office, but little bubbles kept surfacing from my subconscious and bursting in my head—A locked garage?—No suicide note?—Headaches?—In the rear seat?—No hosepipe?—Songs on the telephone?

I didn't tell Sheila about the song when I went home, but I did suggest that we have Doc Macintyre round for a meal the next evening. Now I'd heard Tracy's version of his evidence I wanted to hear what he would say about it.

CHAPTER SIX

'I didn't think that old Capstick was very interested'.

Jim Martin was across the desk from me.

He had come in to give me his version of events leading to the BDS strike, and he'd got to the point where Mulvaney had decided to consult the National Secretary of the Union.

'Why was that?'

'Well, he's been losing his grip for quite a while. They reckon he's got health problems and the word is that he'll resign at the next Conference. He kept telling Con Mulvaney that he didn't think it was a national matter, that we ought to be able to sort it out with our own local management'.

'Presumably he knew all the history of the undermanning arguments?'

'Oh yes. Con told him all that, chapter and verse, but Capstick seemed to blame a lot of it on us'.

'How do you mean?'

'Well, he said that things were bad between us and management at BDS because of loads of wildcat strikes'.

'And had there been?'

'Oh yes, but they weren't our fault. Quite the opposite. For years the Union was a bad joke at BDS. It never did a damn thing about anything. It never held elections. When Shop Stewards left it never replaced them so that there was no proper chain of representation. It got so bad in the end that the Personnel Manager appointed himself as the Branch Secretary'.

'You're joking!'

He shook his head. 'Oh no, I'm not. The Secretary had retired and nobody held an election to replace him, so the Personnel Manager just announced that he'd run the Branch and started calling himself the Branch Secretary'.

'Didn't anyone try to stop him?'

'Nobody cared enough by then. As far as most people were concerned the Union was a dead letter. It would have died out completely, but BDS didn't want a reputation as a non-union firm. They have to do business with governments of any kind, so a non-union plant wouldn't look good to a Labour government, would it?'

'I suppose not. And this was when the wildcat strikes started?'

'Yes. People just hadn't any use for a union that never did or said anything, so when things went wrong you got whole departments and shops just walking out. Then Con Mulvaney came along'.

'He changed things, I gather from Mohammed?'

'He certainly did. Con's a lifelong Union man from Merseyside. When he turned up, he was appalled by the way the Union was. He went to the Personnel Manager and told him he could hand the Secretary's job back, that there was going to be an election'.

'Which he won?'

'Easy. Only about fifteen people turned up

and if Con wanted the job he could have it. But once he'd got it he started straightening things out. He made sure that there was a Shop Steward in every department—that's how I got into it. He nagged me to take on the Shop Stewardship in Computers. Then he started trying to stop the walkouts—the wildcat strikes'.

'Did it work?'

'In the end. He had a bit of a bad time at first, because a lot of people thought he'd just got himself elected for the title, but after a bit they caught on that if they'd got a genuine grievance he'd take it up with the bosses, so they started putting things through the Union'.

'And what happened then?'

'Well, BDS didn't like it, funnily enough. They knew where they were with the wildcats—a few hours production lost and a threat to sack anyone who wasn't back on his next shift and that was it. It'd all be over with nothing given. When Con took over they had arguments and work-to-rules and the things. Con made them follow the safety regulations—the place was full of safety hazards—and they didn't like it 'cos it cost them money. Then they started the undermanning business and he gave them an argument from the start'.

'But he didn't succeed?'

'No. They let two hundred blokes go last year and things were looking really dodgy, but then the Retaliator came up and we all thought it was going to be OK, but instead of taking on more people, they just got into this nonsense of taking in casuals and swapping people about. All we could get out of them was that it was a "regrettable necessity" and that we'd all got to help out and pull together until the Retaliator contract was secure'.

'But surely, they were getting paid to research and develop Retaliator, weren't they? They weren't just doing it on spec?'

'Of course not. But they kept saying that the R and D payments weren't big enough, that we'd have to produce some results for them to get any more cash out of the government'.

'And was there a problem with that?'

'Well, yes, there was'. He paused. 'I don't know how much I'm supposed to tell you about this—nothing probably. Retaliator's the toppest Top Secret'.

'Don't worry about it. I may not be bound by the Official Secrets Act but I am bound by client confidentiality. The Law Society'll throw me out if they catch me selling secrets'.

'Well, Retaliator's a cruise-type weapon. It has a map in its memory of where it's going and what it's going to hit, and all the time it's flying, it scans the ground to compare what's in its head with the terrain and keep itself on target'.

'Right', I said and nodded.

'The other thing is that it's deadly fast.

That's its whole point, really, that it's so fast it'll knock the enemy out before they can hit us'.

I nodded again.

'Well, those two things cause a problem. If you want the best scanning and comparison, it needs to have as much time as possible and to be highly manoeuvrable, but if you want the fastest speed, it has to be flying the simplest path possible, because the greater the speed the more difficult it is to steer it accurately. Follow me?'

'Yes', I said. 'Retaliator has to be fast and manoeuvrable and carry out subtle scanning and correct its own path at high speed'.

'Right. Now we soon had a brilliant scanning system and steering software—the fastest there is, but the steering system could handle it. If the scanning system said "Right ninety degrees" when it was at full speed, that put too much strain on the steering motors and it could misbehave. Sometimes it would throw it so far out it could lose its target entirely and self-destruct. The fact was that BDS had sold an idea to the government without actually being sure it could be done'.

He paused and I nodded again. 'So, having sold the idea in theory, they had trouble making it work in practice'.

'That's right. We had everything working fine here in Belston, but the steering motors were done at Coventry and they were having trouble'.

'And did they have industrial problems at Coventry? Was the Union active there?'

'Not so's you'd notice. We'd got everything running right and on time here, but Coventry was getting all the money and all the manpower to sort out their problems. That was another thing people didn't like'.

'And Capstick wasn't very interested in your troubles?'

'He told me and Con that it was purely a little local difficulty and that it didn't warrant the involvement of the National Secretary. In the end, after we'd argued with him for hours, he agreed to send the Assistant Secretary up to talk to BDS'.

He stopped and shook his head slowly.

'That turned out to be the worst day's work ever'.

'Why was that?'

'Because the bastard sold us out, that's why!'

CHAPTER SEVEN

I still hadn't got the whole of Martin's story when time ran out on us and I had to see somebody else. Kath McBride had got my message and come in again. She settled her large frame in a chair, deposited her handbag on the edge of my desk, lit a cigarette and eyed me, thoughtfully.

'So you didn't believe me?' she began truculently.

I could see this interview going very badly, so I came out at once, surrendering.

'Mrs McBride', I said. 'It's not my place to believe or disbelieve you. It's my job to listen to what you have to tell me and do the best I can with it. Now, that includes trying to see if other people—officials and courts for example—will believe what you have to say. Because, if they won't, we're not going to get anywhere. Now, when you told me how the Coroner's Officer behaved I had difficulty, because I know the bloke and he's usually as smooth as butter, but I've listened to what Tracy Walton had to say about him and she agrees with you—that he was right over the top and determined to keep Sylvia Wellington out of the picture. Why that was I can't say. Maybe he owes Mr Wellington a favour and wanted to keep the girl clear of an inquest. If that was it—or whatever reason he had—he was wrong. If you thought I was disbelieving you, I apologise, Mrs McBride'.

She eyed me silently for a while, less truculently I hoped.

'Well', she said at last, 'I suppose I was a bit upset when I saw you. Perhaps I didn't sound so very convincing. But it doesn't rest with me, Mr Tyroll. Tracy was there, you've heard what she can say and she'd be a witness for me if needed'.

I nodded. 'A good one', I said. 'Now, Mrs McBride, Tracy said something about songs on the phone. What was that about?'

'Not songs', she said. 'Always the same song'.

'What's been happening then?'

'It started just after the Inquest. About three or four nights after. I'd put Eileen—that's my little lass—to bed, and I was sitting with the telly. It would have been about eleven o'clock when the phone went. When I answered it there was no one there at first, no voice like. Then some music started up, like someone playing a tape on the phone. Then it stopped in the middle and the phone cut off'.

'Did you 1471 it?'

She nodded. 'I did that, but it was a suppressed number. Then it happened again, a few nights later'.

'Is it always at the same time?'

'It's usually about eleven o'clock or later, but once or twice it's happened in the day'.

'And it's always the same song?'

She reached into her handbag and found an audiocassette.

'There it is', she said, laying the cassette on my desk. 'I've taped it three times on there. It's always the same'.

I took a cassette recorder from my desk drawer and slotted the tape in. When I switched on there was a distorted fragment of music as the tape came up to speed, a flute or clarinet playing a slow, plaintive melody, then a strong female voice began to sing:

> 'My young love said to me, "My mother won't mind,
> And my father won't slight you for your lack of kind",
> Then she stepped away from me, and this she did say,
> "It will not be long, love, till our wedding day"'.
>
> Then she stepped from my side and she moved through the fair,
> And so fondly I watched her move here and move there,
> And then she went homeward, with one star awake,
> As the swan in the evening moves over the lake'.

The instruments took up a decoration between the verses, and the voice began a third verse but suddenly there was a ragged, ripping sound and the music stopped. I listened to the other two recordings. They were identical.

When I looked back to Mrs McBride she was holding out two sheets of paper.

'I didn't know if you'd know the song', she said, 'so I wrote it all out for you. There's the two verses on the tape and another two'.

I took the paper and read the remaining two verses:

> 'All the people were saying that there's no two are wed,
> But the one has a secret that never is shared,
> So she stepped away from me, with her goods and her gear,
> And that was the last that I saw of my dear.
>
> Till last night she came to me, my dead love came in,
> And so softly she came that her feet made no din.
> She laid her hand on me, and this she did say,
> "It will not be long, love, till our wedding day".

Each of the recordings had been stopped at the second line of the third verse—'But the one has a secret that never is shared'.

'"She Moved Through The Fair"', I said. 'My mother used to sing it. Was it a favourite of Sean's? Has it some connection with him?'

She shook her head. 'Not particularly', she said. 'He knew it, of course, but it wasn't anything special to him'.

'What do you think it means to the person who's playing it?'

'Well, it's about a lad who wants to marry a

girl who's better than him, and he's worried about what her parents'll think of him. That's my Sean and the Wellington girl. Old Wellington would never have been happy with his darling daughter marrying a lad who worked in a garage and lived on a Council estate'.

I nodded. 'But in the song they're going to marry but she dies for some secret reason. When she tells him they'll soon be married, she knows she's going to die. It's the girl who dies, not the boy'.

'Oh, sure, but in the last part he's grieving for her and her ghost comes to him and tells him that it's alright, that they'll soon be wed in any case, which I suppose means that he's going to die as well'.

'Right', I agreed, 'but that's common in folk songs, you know that. There's a lot of songs about lovers grieving for their dead sweethearts and longing to be with them—"The Unquiet Grave", "Lowlands Away", all sorts'.

She smiled for the first time. 'You certainly know your folk songs, Mr Tyroll', she said.

'From my mother', I explained. 'She made her living singing them when I was small, and she used to sing "She Moved Through The Fair", though she only sang three verses. I've never heard that fourth verse'.

'That's the way I learned it', she said, 'and I think it's meant to be about Sean and Sylvia

Wellington'.

'Well, the beginning fits', I said, 'but after that it goes astray. The girl dies—not the boy—and she dies of some illness, presumably. Then the boy dies later, out of grief, I suppose. It's not parallel to Sean and Sylvia after the beginning'.

'Perhaps it's the best he could find', she suggested.

'He?' I queried.

'Him as plays the tape to me'.

'You know who it is?'

'I'm pretty certain, yes', she said. 'I think it's Charlie Nesbit'.

'What makes you think that?'

'Charlie and Sean was at school together—up at Saint Joseph's. They were in a band that they had up there, playing folk dances and that, and the school had some records of Irish songs that they used to play in the intervals. I'm almost certain that "She Moved Through The Fair" was one of them records'.

'But why would he be doing it?'

'He's trying to say something that he won't come out with, Mr Tyroll, that's what'.

'And what do you think that is?'

'It always stops at the bit about a secret. I think he's trying to say there's something secret about Sean's death and it's got to do with the girl'.

I looked at her thoughtfully. I had badly misjudged this woman once and I didn't want to do so again. I wasn't anywhere near so sure as she was about the connection with the song, but I couldn't make any better ones and I had to take account of her beliefs.

'Leave that cassette with me, if you will, Mrs McBride. I need to think about it. In the meantime, whenever it happens again, record it and try to 1471 the call. You never know, we might get lucky. He might forget to suppress his number sooner or later'.

CHAPTER EIGHT

The weather had cooled slightly, but it was still a warm August evening when I arrived home. Sheila was on the patio again, with no guitar but a glass of something that looked cool.

I dropped into a chair. 'Hi!' I said, 'what about a drink for the workers?'

'The workers', she said, 'have been slaving in the kitchen to prepare a feast fit for Doc Macintyre, and don't get settled there because he'll be here soon. Go and change'.

I grabbed the bottle and poured myself a long one.

'Australian wine', I said as it went down my throat.

'Nothing wrong with that', she said, 'and you only guessed it because there's a screwtop on the bottle'.

'What are you going to do in Oz, now that your bottles have screwtops?' I asked.

'What d'you mean?' she said, suspiciously.

'Well, if you put screwtops around your hats to keep the flies off, aren't they going to rattle?'

She scowled. 'Go and change!' she commanded.

'Don't nag', I said.

'I wasn't nagging. I was merely delivering good advice—firmly'.

'And repetitively', I said. 'That's nagging. It used to be a crime'.

She raised an eyebrow. 'Not even the Brits could make that a crime'.

'Ah, but they did. Nagging or scolding was a crime till quite recently'.

'What was the penalty?'

'A nagging woman—a "scold" as they were called—could be put in the stocks, or have her head locked into an iron cage with a mechanism to stop her tongue moving and be led around the town as a dreadful example. Or she could be ducked on a ducking stool or whipped'.

'You're talking about the Middle Ages', she said.

I shook my head. 'That was the law until 1961'.

'What happened then?'

'Ah, well, then the Permissive Society came along and if you wanted to lock women in iron cages and beat them you had to pay for it'.

'Stop talking nonsense and go and change. If Doc comes and sees you in a suit, he'll think you're going to charge him'.

'I wear this rig', I said, 'because careful sociological examination has proved that the British public prefers to be advised and guided by people wearing a collar and tie'.

'Humph!' she snorted. 'Sociologists are a bunch of superstitious parasites, who take the carefully garnered work of social historians and extrapolate it into ludicrous generalities. Go and change!'

'I think I'll go and change', I said and fled.

When I came back, Doc Macintyre was sprawled in a chair on the patio, wineglass in hand, and Sheila was loading the table with enough grub to feed a regiment.

The old Scotsman is a good friend of mine and, over the years, has taught me all I know about dead and injured people. He has a profound knowledge of his subject and lives for the mortuary, good food and malt whisky.

We ate hard for a while, until Doc eased himself in his chair and announced that he couldn't take another mouthful.

'That's a shame', Sheila remarked. 'There's a summer pudding with a drop in it'.

His eyes lit up again. 'He can't have that', I said. 'He'll get nicked driving home'.

'It's a fine night. I'll walk', he announced. 'Anyway, I'll say that someone spiked my orange juice'.

I laughed. 'I can just see you telling the Magistrates that you drink orange juice. You'd get done for perjury as well'.

'Well then, I'll tell them I was led astray by an alcoholic summer pudding'. By this time a large portion had appeared in front of him.

'Won't work', I said. 'Somebody's already tried that one. DPP—v—Wynne. Not a summer pudding but three slices of Christmas cake that put her over the limit. The magistrates found it a special reason not to disqualify her, but the Court of Appeal sent it back, said the story was preposterous, so I don't suppose summer pudding'd work either'.

'Then I'll walk', he repeated, finishing the pudding swiftly.

Another portion went the same way before he leaned back from the table again.

'Now, young Tyroll', he began. 'Time was when you were a married man whose wife would not give me house room because she thought that talk of dead folk was disgusting. Then you were divorced and used regularly to invite me to share a takeaway by way of relieving your bachelor state. Now you have a beautiful and intelligent fiancée and only allow her to invite me to feed when you want to pick my brains. What is it this time? Have you stumbled across another murder? Inspector Parry's always complaining that you two keep finding murders that he has to explain'.

'I don't think so', I said, 'but it's peculiar. Tell me about suicide'.

'I've thought about it', he said. 'Who hasna?'

'Not you', I said. 'Suicides in general'.

'It's a growth industry', he said. 'About ten young men a day commit suicide in Britain'.

'As many as that?' I asked. 'Young men?'

'Aye, and about half as many women, but mostly young men'.

'Why do they do it?'

He looked at me in amazement for a moment.

'How the blazes would I know? My patients don't talk to me'.

'Come on, Doc', said Sheila, 'You must have pretty good ideas about the whys and wherefores'.

'Everybody does it, lassie. All manner of folks commit suicide. Young folk do it because they're lovelorn or they've got sexual problems or exam problems; middle-aged folk do it because they're lovelorn or they've got sexual problems or they've got money worries; old folk do it because they're lonely or poor or depressed'.

'Who doesn't do it?'

'Healthy, well-balanced people, with a realistic view of life's wee ups and downs, and people whose religion makes it a sin'.

'Like Catholics?'

'Like Catholics', he agreed. 'Was she a

Catholic?'

'He was a Catholic', I said. 'You say that all sorts of people do it because they're lovelorn. What about people who are in love?'

'Don't be daft', he said. 'Being in love is the biggest kick in the world. People stop smoking when they're in love; they take to writing songs and poetry; they bathe more often and tidy up regularly. Depression's the disease of being human. Being in love is the only guaranteed cure'.

'What about being in love with someone you can't marry?'

He shook his shaggy head. 'Doesna usually end in suicide', he said. 'Divorces, runaway romances, Gretna Green weddings, even murder sometimes, but not often suicide'.

'What about people who are ill—or who think they're ill?' asked Sheila.

'Was he ill? If he knew he'd got something fatal, maybe, though not often. Cancer, AIDS, they don't make people do it. They hang on to life. People with the chronic diseases, they're the same—they hang on. What had your fellow got?'

'Headaches', I said.

'Headaches!' he exploded. 'If everybody who had a headache topped themselves, they'd be bringing truckloads into my wee mortuary'.

'Do they always leave notes?'

'Mostly. Not always. A lot of folk do it to get their own back on somebody, so they want to be sure they've made their point, so they leave a note, saying, "Dear Ethel, I cannot live without you a day longer". That's supposed to make Ethel feel bad about the fact that she's run off to the Seychelles with the rent man'.

I nodded. 'What methods do people use?'

'Painless ones, usually. It usetae be the gas oven till North Sea gas came in. Now everybody's got a medicine cabinet with enough painkillers to wipe out a herd of buffalo, so it's often an overdose. Sometimes it's a gun, if they've got one. Occasionally it's slit wrists in the bath, but not very often. That takes a certain amount of cold nerve. Then there's exotic ones with fancy ideas—they're usually men. Women take the soft options'.

'Like what fancy ideas?' asked Sheila.

'There was a fellow once who took his lawnmower extension lead, stripped off, stood in his garden pond and jabbed the bare end of the lead up his bottom'.

'What happened?'

'Well, he got a few nasty burns in some strange places and all his puir bloody goldfish were killed. If you're going to do it, keep it simple, laddie'.

'What about car exhausts?'

'Aye. They're quite popular. The modern version of the gas oven'.

'Do they always put a hose in the exhaust?'

'Usually. Otherwise it takes longer, unless it's a very small garage.

'Do they sit in the front or back seat, Doc?' asked Sheila.

'In the front—always. It's their car for Heaven's sake and they're going to die in it, so they sit in the driver's seat'.

'What about one who didn't?'

'Didna what?'

'Sit in the front seat. He was sitting in the back seat and the front passenger seat was out on the garage floor'.

He looked at me sharply. 'You're talking about that laddie off the Wednesfield Road a couple of months ago. What was his name?—McBride, aye, that's it'.

I nodded. 'That's the one. You were at the Inquest. What do you think?—Suicide, accident, murder?'

'I don't know', he said.

CHAPTER NINE

It had grown dark, but it was still warm. We sat in the light from the windows, Sheila and I looking at Mac. I had been relying on the experienced old pathologist to put an end to my doubts about Sean McBride's death, and to do so on a solid factual basis. Instead, he had laid his doubts on top of mine.

In the silence he hunched forward, taking his whisky glass in both hands and gazing into it as though it were a scrying glass.

'Tell me', he said, 'what you know about young McBride's death—just the facts, none of your lawyers' opinions and possibilities'.

He remained hunched over his glass while I recited what I knew of the case. He half-closed his eyes and nodded occasionally as I mentioned something that he remembered. When I had done, he looked up, reached for the bottle and poured his glass full, taking a long sip before he spoke.

'Sean McBride', he began at last, 'was a perfectly healthy eighteen-year-old, so far as I could see. All his organs were healthy. There were no lesions or tumours of the brain to account for any headaches. I was told that the body had been found in a lock-up garage off the Wednesfield Road, slumped in the rear seat of his car. Examination of the blood established the cause of death as carbon monoxide poisoning. I was told that there was no hosepipe from the exhaust.

'Examination of the lungs showed that there had not been—there was no soot in the lungs. I was also told that there was no suicide note, that the garage door was locked and that only the boy had a key to it. On those facts I would not say suicide, though it might be. I would most probably say accident'.

'What kind of an accident?' I asked.

'I was shown photographs of the scene', he said, 'and, as you say, the body was sprawled in the rear seat with the left foot in the space where the front passenger seat normally fits. That seat had been removed and was standing away from the car. It seemed to me that there was only one reason for the removal of the seat and the position of the body'.

He sipped his drink while we waited. 'Sex', he said at last. 'Young McBride had been engaged in what, in my youth, we called the "Backseat Foxtrot", hence the removal of the seat and the body being in the back instead of the front'.

We nodded. 'Right', I said, 'that makes sense, but . . .'

'It more than makes sense', he said. 'Because the body was not found for days I couldn't fix a precise time of death, but I could say that he had had sexual activity shortly before he died. It leaves physical and chemical indications and it's a routine check in dealing with a dead youngster'.

'You never said that before the Coroner', I said.

'No, I didnae, and that was because I was most particularly asked not to'.

'Who by?' asked Sheila.

'By the Coroner's Officer. He explained to me that the boy had been having an affair with Tom Wellington's schoolgirl daughter and that it would only cause grief and attract unnecessary publicity if I mentioned it. I had no problem with that. Strictly speaking it wasn't the Coroner's business. Under the Statute of Coronary his function is to enquire into how a dead person came to be one, not what they were doing when they were alive. I can tell you something else, as well. McBride and the girl—or a girl—had been using that garage regularly as a trysting place'.

'You couldn't tell that from the body', I said.

'No, I couldnae, but I could tell it from the photographs. Along the side of the car was a litter of used condoms'.

'So', I said, 'Sean's reason for going to the garage was an assignation with Sylvia Wellington and they had sex, but how do you reckon that he came to die by accident?'

'They did their business', he said, 'and she went home. If it was Sylvie Wellington she wouldnae stay out late. Daddy would never stand for it. She slipped away home and left him sitting in the love seat. He lit a cigarette and stayed there—there were fag ends on the floor of the car and one burned down between his fingers. He also ran the engine to warm himself. It was a chilly night'.

'Was it?'

'Aye. The nights were chilly all that weekend. I checked with Edgbaston Observatory. Anyway, he ran the motor, the fumes built up and he died quietly'.

'Why did he run the motor in a closed space? He was garage mechanic—he must have known the risk?' asked Sheila.

'I don't know', he said, testily. 'You'll be asking me next why he was wearing white underpants and not blue yins! That meets most of the evidence and doesnae contradict anything. Perhaps he asked her to leave the door a wee bit open and she didn't, who knows. But it was an accident, you mark my words'.

'You could have said that at the Inquest', I remarked.

'Aye, so I could and what good would that have done. His poor bloody mother has three choices—suicide, accident or murder. If it's suicide she has to live with the idea that he was so unhappy he killed himself; if it was accident she has to live with the fact that his death was totally pointless. At least if it was murder there's a villain behind it, one who can be caught and punished. Why would I tell her it was an accident, when I don't have to?'

'You crafty old bugger! You always thought it was an accident. You checked with the Observatory', Sheila said.

Mac eyed me sadly. 'Why d'ye have to take up with clever lasses?' he asked.

'Because they're the first to spot my attractions. Anyway, my ex-wife wasn't very clever, so that's only one out of two'.

Sheila laid a firm hand on my arm. 'And there isn't going to be a third', she announced.

'You're that sure?' said Mac.

'Too right I am! If I suspect anything, he'll

suddenly predecease me'.

'Anyway', I said, 'getting back to where we were—you're sure it was an accident?'

'It's the simplest explanation, Chris, and the simplest explanation is usually the right one'.

'Not always', I said, and got up to go indoors.

I brought Kath McBride's tape and a cassette player back to the table. I told them about the phone calls and I played them the whole of the tape. All three of us sat in silence while the plaintive old air floated over the dark garden.

'Sounds like Delia Murphy', said Mac when the music ended. I switched off.

'Who's she?' asked Sheila.

'She was an Irish singer from before your time. Wife of the Irish Minister to Australia. Made records of sentimental Irish ballads, "The Spinning Wheel", "Three Lovely Lasses From Bannion" and that. She probably did "She Moved Through The Fair". It certainly sounds like her'.

'Does it matter who she is?' said Sheila. 'What's it mean?'

She looked at me. I shook my head. 'You tell me. I don't know. Perhaps it means he was murdered'.

'It means somebody thinks he knows something about it, anyway', Mac said.

'Why that song?' asked Sheila.

We went at it. As the moon came up we sat

around and argued every reasonable and many unreasonable theories about the song. It turned cold and we moved indoors for coffee, still arguing. Mac wandered deep into Celtic folklore and the significance of swans, I argued the differences between events in the song, Sheila kept coming back to the point at which the recording ended.

'It's the same tape being played on each call', she said. 'It's been recorded from an old-fashioned disc—you can hear someone taking the pick-up off. So, there's a deliberate choice to end at that point in the song. It has to mean something'.

'Then it's emphasising the reference to a secret', I said.

'But what secret can it be? A secret between Sean and the girl? A secret about Sean and the girl? A secret about how he died?'

We gave up and the Doc rang for a cab. As it arrived and he stood up to go a thoughtful expression crossed his face.

'In the song the girl dies and comes back for the boy. It was the boy who died in reality. Does that mean that the girl's next? Is that what it's saying?'

CHAPTER TEN

The morning mail in the office brought a letter on an unfamiliar letterhead. My client Samson had given me a plain name and an address in Shropshire as the details of the landowner who had nicked the ponies belonging to Samson and his pals, but the reply was on the notepaper of something called 'The Maiden Group'.

The interests listed on the heading were varied and impressive—construction, freight haulage, vehicle hire, security—even leisure and entertainment. The owner of all this profitable activity was the landowner, Dennis Maiden, whose vigorous signature was scrawled under a short, blunt text. It said:

'Re: Trespass by Ponies—Thank you for your letter. I am not prepared to let my field to your clients. I enclose my bill for their use of my land and for my expenses in rounding-up and removing the animals. If this sum is not paid within seven days, I shall dispose of the animals as I think fit'.

Well, he was quite entitled not to let his field if he didn't want to, and his charges for grazing were perfectly reasonable. It was the second part of the bill that raised my hackles. It seemed that it had taken two drivers, two hired vehicles and six other men, a total of six hours to travel to the field, round up two tame ponies and transport them to wherever they were. Since it had been done on a Sunday, all these men had been paid at double-time, and none of them were casual labourers. You might have thought that an enterprise as big as the Maiden Group could have found a few blokes who'd like to earn a few quid on a Sunday, but it seemed not. The labour employed had been a crane-driver, a bulldozer driver, a security supervisor and assorted craftsmen—very well-paid craftsmen by the look of their double-time rates.

It was a blatant try-on and it made me angry—so angry that, without thinking much about the accessibility of the owners of fat companies, I snatched up the phone and punched out the Wolverhampton number at the top of the letter.

By the time the number was ringing I realised that I was going to end up being bounced around the Maiden Group's switchboard and end up leaving a message with a secretary. I was wrong. To my surprise I was quickly connected to the man himself.

'Dennis Maiden', said a strong Black Country voice.

I introduced myself and said that I'd received his letter.

'So, when can I expect your cheque?' he said.

I gritted my teeth. 'My clients', I said, 'are

quite willing to pay your reasonable charges for the period that the animals grazed on your land, and I've no quarrel with the amount you suggest...'

'It's not a suggestion. It's a demand', he interrupted.

I gritted my teeth again. 'Very well', I said. 'I've no wish to argue about the grazing charge, but your expenses for rounding-up the animals are completely over the top. Added to which, the local police knew whose ponies they were. All you had to do was contact my clients and ask them to shift the animals'.

'And what security would I have had then to make them pay for the use of my field?' he demanded. 'Look, Mr Tyroll, I know who your clients are. They're a bunch of bloody hamefilers and snaffle-bangers. They can give themselves airs by buying cheap ponies for their kids, but when it comes down to it, they haven't got a spare penny. I wanted to secure my grazing rent, so I took the animals. Are you trying to tell me that I can't seize the ponies for debt?'

'No', I said, and by now my teeth were permanently gritted. 'I'm just saying that it was unnecessary. You might have tried trusting my clients'.

He gave a quick barking laugh. 'Trusted them, eh?' he said. 'I didn't build the Maiden Group by trusting people'.

'Very well', I said. 'You had the right to

seize the animals if you chose to do so, but it didn't have to cost as much as you claim. They're only two little girls' ponies, after all, not two wild stallions. One man and a truck could have done it easily'.

'I had to call for volunteers', he said, 'and I had to warn them of the dangers...'

'Dangers?' I cut in. 'The dangers of rounding up two ponies in a little field?'

'If you'd ever had a horse's hoof in your bollocks, you'd know about the dangers', he said. 'One of my lads might have got maimed. As to the cost, I had to use the people who volunteered and that's who they were. I couldn't pay them less than I'd have paid them for doing their own job on a Sunday afternoon'.

'You have an obligation at law to mitigate your loss', I said.

He snorted. 'Mitigate my loss? What's that supposed to mean? I wondered when we'd get down to the legal argy-bargy'.

'It means', I said, 'that you can't claim unnecessary expense against my clients. A court won't allow it'.

'It ay going to go into any court', he said. 'I told you—I know about Samson and his mates. They ay got the kind of cash as can go up against me, have they? The three of them ay got a pot to piss in nor a window to throw it out of. They've got two choices—they can pay up and have their ponies back, or they can argue. If they argue, I'll sell the bloody ponies for dogsmeat'.

'I'm sure my client's daughter and her friend will be delighted to hear that', I said.

'Oh, don't you try and turn the sentiment on', he said. 'I've got a daughter and she rides. More than a bit, she's a champion in the showring, but every one of her horses she's paid for—even the first. She worked odd jobs and saved her money when she was at school to buy her first pony. You tell your Samson and his snaffle-bangers as they can pay my bill in full or I'll send the ponies back in cans and they can buy their lasses a pup each'.

With which kindly thought he put the phone down on me.

I was just about to hurl Stone's "Justices' Manual" out of the window, volume by volume, when the door opened and the smiling face of my assistant, Alasdair Thayne, looked in.

'You're back', I said, gracelessly.

'As you see', he said. 'Fit as a fiddle and raring to go. Do I take it you're not having a good morning, governor?'

'Have you ever come across Dennis Maiden?' I asked.

'Dennis Maiden? The Maiden Group? Building, haulage, vehicle hire and all that? The bloke who's always giving money to local charities?'

'The very same', I said, 'except that the

arrogant, miserable bastard hasn't got a single charitable cell in his wretched body'.

'You lost the argument?' he said.

'I'm used to rich and powerful people going about treading on people and doing what they please', I said, 'but this one rubs your face in it. He's just told me that he can do what he likes because our clients haven't got enough money to stop him'.

'Then you want some law', he said.

'Law?' I said. 'If you can find me a piece of law that says I can have Dennis bloody Maiden put in the stocks and whipped by the Parish Clerk six times a day, I'll do it'.

He shook his head. 'No stocks left', he said.

'Oh yes there are—in the museum. You find me the law and I'll personally pay for a replica—with spikes'.

He nodded thoughtfully and left without a word.

CHAPTER ELEVEN

It did not get better. The day clouded over, the rain started to fall and every idiot and nuisance on my files decided to call me. At five o'clock I called it a day, rang for a cab and went home.

Sheila must be psychic. Despite the fact that it was my turn in the kitchen, she welcomed me with food, coffee, alcohol, and only the most minimal conversation until I had eaten, drunk and unwound.

'I am going', I announced eventually, 'to pass this evening watching telly. If a client rings in deep distress or dire peril, tell them that I'm out, ill, in jail, dead or whatever'.

I picked up the local paper to look for the TV schedule. Kath McBride's face, made paler and wider as news photos do, stared solemnly at me from the front page, alongside a headline that said, "Phone Fiend Harasses Grieving Mum".

I swore and read the accompanying story. It told me nothing I didn't know, merely recited the tale of the mystery phone calls. It referred to Sean as, "her 18-year-old son, who sadly committed suicide in a fume-filled garage only weeks ago".

I passed the paper to Sheila and picked up the phone to ring Kath. As soon as she heard me she became apologetic.

'I know what you're going to say, Mr Tyroll', she said. 'I didn't put it in the paper, well, not deliberately'.

'How did it get in there, then?'

'I was talking to this fellow at the Club last night. Really sympathetic, he seemed, but it turned out he was a reporter. Has it done any harm?'

'If Charlie Nesbit was making those calls, that story may make him duck and hide. In fact, whoever was making them may do the same. I think I'd better go and see Charlie before he disappears. What's his address?'

She gave me the address—not far from the garage where Sean had died—and I rang off. Sheila was picking up her handbag.

'Want a chauffeur?'

'If you're up for it. Here comes the rotten end of a rotten day'.

The "place" in the address Kath had given me was what used to be called a "close" because it had a dead end. Blocking that end was a square, redbrick building with a concrete balcony along its front and a stairway at the lefthand end. I wondered if le Corbusier would have bothered if he could have known where minimalism and functionalism would take modern architecture. Kath had said that Nesbit's flat was on the ground floor at the back. We left the car and followed a concrete path around the side of the block. It turned across the rear of the building, flanking a grey, dusty patch of yard, ornamented with steel clothes-line posts and plastic wheelie bins. Three doors painted in sunfaded Municipal Green and three small kitchen windows looked out on to the yard. Nesbit's door was the far one.

I rang the bell vigorously, hearing no ringing from inside and wondering whether it was working. Whichever, it produced no response. I rattled the flap of the letter-box loudly with equally little result. At last I tried the door and found it was unlocked.

I always hate this bit. The law says that anyone can come to your door, knock on it or ring your bell, for any legitimate reason. If they don't have legal authority to be there, you can always tell them to "Bugger off" and they must comply. If you don't answer the door and it isn't locked, that isn't an invitation to enter. The moment you do that, you're trespassing and the penalty will depend on why you're trespassing.

I stepped inside cautiously, calling Nesbit's name and motioning to Sheila to stay on the doorstep. There was no hall, the front door opened straight into a sitting room and a small kitchen opened on the left. The room was lit by a window at the far side, alongside which another door led, presumably to the bedroom and bathroom. The room smelt of stale smoke, food and socks.

Sheila followed me in and sniffed the air. 'Strewth!' she said, 'Eau de bachelor—industrial strength!'

I called a couple more times, while I surveyed the sitting room. Two walls were shelved and the shelves untidily crammed with paperback books and records. An old-fashioned hi-fi stood beneath the shelves and a large colour TV with a cheap video-recorder alongside it. An acoustic guitar and a tenor banjo were propped in a corner.

There was still no response to my calls, so I stepped through the far door. A small hall gave access to a bedroom on the left and the bathroom to the right. An open door showed that the bedroom held only an unmade double bed and a cluttered dressing table. The bathroom door was shut.

I hate this bit, too. Last time I stepped into a stranger's bathroom, I found him hanging from the shower-head. I tapped the bathroom door, called Nesbit's name again, then went in.

A slim young man clad in grubby denims was doubled over the side of the bath, his head and his left arm inside it. His right hand trailed on the bath mat and close to it lay a small automatic pistol. If this was Charlie Nesbit, a single shot had passed through his head and he was very dead.

Sheila was examining the records when I returned to the sitting room. She turned to show me a 78 rpm disc in a heavy cardboard sleeve. The punched-out sleeve centre showed the label—'Bridget Reilly—She Moved Thro' The Fair'.

'Good', I said, 'but that isn't the problem any more'.

She noted my face. 'He's dead', she guessed.

I nodded. 'Have you got your mobile phone?'

She took it from her shoulder-bag and handed it over,

'While I phone the police', I said, 'fetch the

camera from the glove compartment'.

'The fuzz'll photograph it', she said.

'Yes, but they won't give them to me, so we might as well take advantage. Just don't touch anything more'.

I didn't call 999. I rang John Parry's mobile. He answered quickly.

'John? Chris Tyroll. Are you on duty? Good. Sheila and I have run into a spot of police business in Wheatstone Place'.

'What sort of police business? Not another corpse?'

'Well, as a matter of fact, yes'.

There was a muffled explosion of oaths in Welsh and English at the other end, ending in '. . . attract them like flies to bloody jam'. Then, 'Indoors or outdoors?'

I explained the situation in outline. 'Right!' he said, 'Get out and sit in the car. Don't touch anything in the flat or I'll kill you. Don't even breathe until you're out of the door. I'll be right there'.

He wasn't quite 'right there'. He left me ample time to photograph the whole interior of Nesbit's flat before I retired to the car.

Sheila and I were sitting silent in the car when two police cars hurtled into the close and drew up in front of the block. Inspector Parry unwound himself from the front of one, making a beeline for us and motioning his colleagues to make for Nesbit's flat. He let himself into Sheila's car and settled in the rear seat.

'Right!' he said, 'What unlikely excuse have you got this time for finding another stiff on my patch?'

I expanded the brief story I had given him on the phone, and he listened quietly, nodding occasionally.

'And what's this one, then? Suicide or murder?' he asked when I had finished.

I shook my head. 'Suicide seems the obvious explanation'.

'Why?' he demanded.

'Because he saw the story in tonight's paper'.

'Why would that drive him to suicide?'

'He seemed to have some kind of secret knowledge of Sean McBride's death', I said. 'Or else why the phone calls? If that was very guilty knowledge, he wouldn't want the press drawing attention to it'.

'Are you saying that Nesbit may have killed his mate?"

'I'm saying that I am now entirely convinced that Sean McBride did not commit suicide. If Sean was killed, then someone did it and that someone could reasonably have been Charlie Nesbit. After all, it's usually friends and relatives who murder people'.

He nodded. 'If you have to find a dead body, Chris, and it seems you can't stop yourself from finding them, do you think you could have found a nice, straightforward suicide, not a possible suicide linked to a suicide that probably wasn't and might have been a murder?'

'Sorry. I just can't bear to think of you getting bored'.

He opened a door and heaved himself out of the car. 'This'll cost you', he said. 'Don't go to bed early. I'll be round for supper'.

As we pulled away I gave Sheila Kath McBride's address. 'We'd better go and give her the bad news', I said, 'before she reads it in the papers'.

Kath was at home in front of the telly. In the dining room her daughter was hunched over the table with a display of homework. Kath saw my face and shut the dining room door.

'What is it?' she said. 'What's happened?'

'It's Charlie', I said. 'What does he look like?'

'He's a thin lad, really skinny, with auburn hair'.

'Then I'm sorry to tell you he's dead', I said.

Both of her fists came up clenched and her pale face turned paler. 'Oh no!' she gasped. 'Oh no! Oh no! Oh no!'

Sheila took her by the shoulders and lowered her into a chair, then disappeared towards the kitchen. I lowered myself onto a couch and sat helplessly, while Kath bent her head and beat her clenched fists against her knees.

At last she looked up, tears streaming down her face. 'I did it!' she declared. 'I did it, with my big mouth. The people who killed Sean have killed poor little Charlie now'.

I shook my head. 'You didn't do it', I said. 'It looks as if it's either suicide or murder. Very probably suicide. Did Charlie own a gun, do you know?'

She stared at me, blankly. 'A gun?' she repeated. 'I don't know. I wouldn't think so. What would he want with a gun? What sort of a gun?'

'A small automatic pistol', I said.

'I never saw him with one and Sean never said anything, but Charlie was a funny one. He made his money ducking and diving, selling a bit of pot and that. Maybe he did have a gun, I don't know'.

Sheila came back with a tray of tea mugs and Kath stirred herself to fetch a bottle from a cabinet and gave each of us a generous splash in the tea. Then we sat silent again and drank our tea.

At length Kath wiped her eyes and looked at us. 'This is the most terrible thing', she said. 'As if my Sean wasn't enough, now it's his poor mate. Who's done it, Mr Tyroll? Who's done it?'

'I've had a long talk with Macintyre, the pathologist', I said. 'He agrees that Sean's death wasn't suicide'.

Kath's eyes widened. 'He says it wasn't

suicide!' she exclaimed. 'So he agrees it was murder?'

'No, no. You're going too fast. He is sure it wasn't suicide, but he can't rule out some kind of accident'.

Her face fell again. 'It was no accident', she said stubbornly.

'Kath', I said, 'I know Charlie's death has made things worse for you, but it has caused one advantage'.

'What's that?' she demanded suspiciously.

'The police will now connect Charlie's death to Sean's'.

'Why would they do that?' she said. 'They always go the soft, easy way'.

'They'll do that', I said, 'because I have pointed them in that direction already'.

'Yes', she said, 'but they'll say, "Ah, the Coroner said suicide, so it must have been"'.

'Ordinarily I'd agree with you, but the officer in Charlie's case is Detective Inspector Parry. John Parry likes to do his job thoroughly, and he'll be looking at both deaths now, which makes things a lot easier'.

'And if he thought there was something wrong about Sean's death, he'd do something about it?' she asked, with understandable suspicion.

'Yes, Kath. He would, and it would be easier for him to get the Inquest re-opened than it would be for us, so keep your fingers crossed'.

I was ready to leave, but Sheila was looking

about her.

'Kath', she said, 'have you cleared Sean's things? Is his room still the way he kept it?'

Kath nodded. 'It is', she said. 'I cannot bring meself to do anything about it. If you want to see it, it's the one opposite the stair-top. I won't come up with you, but you're welcome'.

Sheila glanced at me and got up. I followed her upstairs.

Sean's room was an ordinary, squarish, council-flat bedroom, furnished with a single divan bed, a cabinet, a wardrobe and a chest of drawers. A stereo radio-cassette stood on the floor by the bed and an acoustic guitar hung on a wall. A half-filled holdall lay on the bed. The bag he had been taking away with him. A Chinon camera with a built-in zoom lay on the chest of drawers.

The only striking feature of the room was the photos, which covered every available wallspace, blu-tacked in rows and columns. Colour pictures of Sean and his pals at every kind of event over the past ten years. In many of the more recent was a girl with a pale, oval face, wide dark eyes and long black hair. In all of them Sean looked cheerful. In the ones with the girl, he looked happy. None of them looked like a potential suicide, but then, nor did Charlie Nesbit who was in many of them. Some of the photos showed just three people—Sean and the girl and Charlie. All relaxed, smiling, laughing. And now two were dead.

We checked the wardrobe and the drawers, but found nothing unusual. Sean McBride had lived an ordinary life. Maybe he had died an ordinary—accidental—death. Downstairs again we found that Tracy Walton had arrived and was sitting with Kath McBride. We explained the situation to her and she shook her head silently, then showed us out.

CHAPTER TWELVE

John Parry was as good as his word. He turned up for supper, looking less than his usual cheerful self. We let him eat before the questions started.

'Let me see, now', he said at last, drawing thoughtfully on his coffee. 'You said that the McBride boy's death was either accident or murder, I think?'

I nodded.

'Well, then, this one's different. It's either suicide or murder'.

'It's an equation', said Sheila. 'Sean's death equals accident or murder; Charlie's death equals murder or suicide. Aren't you supposed to add them together?'

We looked at her blankly.

'Add them together', she repeated. 'Sean dead plus Charlie dead equals two murders or an accident and a suicide or a murder and a suicide. If the simplest answer is most likely to be true, then both are murders'.

She stared at us, daring us to argue.

'That's the most brilliant piece of illogicality I've ever heard', said John.

'Oscar Wilde said all the harm in the world was done by people being logical; nobody did any harm by being reasonable. That's reasonable', she announced.

'It's possible', said John, cautiously, 'but where's it come from? Two murders and not even one motive?'

'I thought you blokes didn't bother about motive', she said.

'Well, now', he said, 'we never have to prove a motive, but us old-fashioned coppers always like to have one. It gives us a cosy feeling that we might be right'.

'So why don't we know how Charlie died?' I asked.

'We do. He was shot through the right side of the head with a small bore pistol. A single shot, right through the brain. Question is, who did it? There's no real sign of anyone else on the premises'.

'I'll bet there's no sign of us on the premises', Sheila said, 'but we were there'.

'True', he agreed, 'and I did say "no real sign". You saw the body, Chris. Remember how he was placed?'

'Yes. He was kneeling, bent over the side of

the bath. His left arm was in the bath, also his head and shoulder. His right arm was trailing beside the bath and the pistol was lying near it'.

He nodded. 'What was on the floor?'

'A hard bathroom carpet, I think'.

He nodded again. 'It's up to Doc Macintyre to tell us all about it, but there's a peculiar injury. The left knee of his jeans is slightly torn, the skin's abraded under the tear and there's a little bloodstain on the carpet'.

'What's that mean?' I asked.

'It could mean he was flung down onto his knees and scraped his knee hard on the carpet. There's also a couple of marks on his neck, either side. It just might be that someone seized him by the neck, forced him down by the bath and shot him'.

'But there's no sign of anyone else there?' said Sheila.

'No, indeed', he said. 'But there's no sign of you two either, and you were both there', and he smiled triumphantly.

'The door was unlocked when we arrived', I said.

'Yes. He often left his door unlocked. We've traced him to the local pub in the early afternoon, about two o'clock. Then he left on his own. Doc says that he died not long after judging from the state of rigor mortis. So—suppose he goes home and someone's waiting for him'.

'Where the blazes would they wait?' demanded Sheila. 'There's nowhere to hide in that flat!'

'Ah! But there is. There's one place', said Parry. 'In between the sitting room and the bedroom and bathroom there's a little hall, right?'

I nodded.

'It's blind on the right end, where it leads up to the dividing wall. That's the end by that bathroom door. At the other end—by the bedroom door—there's a built-in cupboard'.

'So what are you saying?' I asked.

'If you knew he was on his way back from the pub, you could walk in and wait in that end of the hall—in front of the cupboard. He comes back from the pub and walks through the sitting room, heading for the bathroom for a pee. He steps into the hallway, turning towards the right. He doesn't see you because you're stood back in the deepest shadow. As he turns, you step out, grab him at the back of the neck, stick a gun in his ribs and shove him into the bathroom, forcing him to kneel and lean over into the bath'.

'Then you shoot him', finished Sheila.

'Unless you want to know something. Then you might ask a question or two before you shoot him'.

'That's very good', I said. 'So you do believe it was murder?'

'No, boyo. I think it could have been, but he

might have come home drunk, spun himself into a fit of misery and gone and kneeled by the bath and ended it all. There's only his prints on the gun'.

'What about the record?' I asked.

'It looks like Mrs McBride was right, that Charlie made the phone calls, but what does that mean? Was he guilty about Sean's death? Did he feel responsible in some way? Was he actually responsible? Did he cause the accident? Did he murder him? All of those would give him a motive for suicide'.

We were running round in circles again. 'Come on, John', I pleaded. 'Gut feelings. What do you feel?'

He pursed his lips and looked into the distance. 'Gut feelings?' he said. 'I don't like the gun. Charlie Nesbit was a small-time dope pedlar. He wasn't mixed up with the big boys. He bought and sold in small quantities on the street. Lads like that don't carry or keep guns. I've looked at his record—no violence of any kind, just petty dishonesty and dope offences'.

The big detective shook his head slowly. 'The gun's not right', he said. 'I can see Charlie Nesbit topping himself. That's not difficult. But not a gun. He'd have taken pills or hanged himself. And the gun itself. It's a brand-new, chrome-plated automatic. Where'd he get it? It's a French weapon. A handbag gun, made for shooting husbands and lovers and pretending it was an accident. Not the kind of thing Charlie Nesbit would have'.

'Then what does your gut say about motive?' I pressed.

He stood up. 'That's the bugger, boyo. I haven't got a gut feeling about motive, apart from the fact that it's to do with Sean McBride. Anyway, I've delivered the official thanks of the Force for finding us yet another body we'd managed to overlook, and I am going home. I have had enough'.

So had I, but I lay awake and smoked after Sheila had gone to sleep. At least, I thought she was asleep until she whispered to me.

'It makes sense, doesn't it?'

'What?' I said, startled.

'Charlie Nesbit knew something secret about Sean's death and he got killed for it'.

'Could be', I said.

'It makes sense of Mac's warning, as well'.

'Mac's warning?'

'About the song,', she said. 'That the song might mean that Sylvia's in danger'.

I had had enough of gut reactions, guesses and twisted logic. Unfortunately Sheila's twisted logic often concealed real intuition.

That kept me awake much longer.

CHAPTER THIRTEEN

There was some good news in the morning. Mac had sent his papers on Sean McBride over to my office, and I was about to go into them when Alasdair arrived, carrying a wide grin.

'We've got him, Guv'nor', he said as he sat down.

'Who?'

'Dennis Maiden. You wanted some law, I've got you some'.

'Tell me', I said.

Alasdair took out his battered tobacco tin and began rolling a cigarette. Why a man who dresses like a thirties film star chooses to smoke like a tramp I've never understood.

'Maiden says', he began, 'that he has the right to take our clients' ponies because our clients trespassed on his land and allowed their ponies to eat his grass. Right?'

'Right'.

'Following from which, he says that our clients owe him the cost of the grazing and the roundup and that entitles him to seize the ponies as security for an unpaid debt. Yes?'

'Right', I said again. 'Don't tell me—you've found some law that says he can't seize the ponies'.

He shook his head and drew on his strange-smelling cigarette. 'No', he said. 'All the law I can find says he can do that, but there's a law which restricts what he can do with them'.

'You mean he can't carry out his threat to have them turned into dog food?'

He shook his head again. 'No, no, not that. The Distress Act says that you can seize a debtor's cattle or horses for debt, but you can't take them more than three miles from where you seized them, nor across a county boundary'.

I stared at him. 'We don't know where they are', I said.

'Oh, yes we do', he said. 'That address that Samson gave you in the first place—Maiden's private address—is his country pad in Shropshire. It's a big spread near my people's place. That's where Maiden actually lives. His daughter lives there, too—Shirley Maiden the showjumper. That's where she keeps her horses. There's a big stable layout there. Where else would he have taken them?'

'Makes sense', I agreed, 'but where does it take us? What's the penalty? Do we get to gallop over his drawbridge with the County Sheriff and loot his castle? Can we dangle him from his own battlements, or massacre his varlets or something?'

'Not quite that dramatic', he said, 'but it's a criminal offence and is fineable for every day that it persists'.

'How much?'

'Five shillings. How much is that in debased coin of the realm?'

'Twenty-five pence', I said. 'Twenty-five pence a day will really worry a man of Maiden's wealth'.

'It was a lot of money back in fifteen-something when the Act was passed. Anyway, it's not the penalty, it's the point. We can make him look stupid and mean'.

I began to like it. I picked up my microphone and started to dictate:

On the Samson file, a letter on headed bond with a copy for Mr Samson and a file copy. Letter is to Mr Dennis Maiden at the office address on his last letter to us. Dear Mr Maiden, comma, paragraph, re colon your illegal seizure of ponies, underline that heading, space. Further to our telephone discussion and your threat to have my clients' ponies destroyed if your exaggerated bill is not met, comma, I write to give you notice that your actions in seizing the animals amount to a criminal offence under the Distress Act, stop. As your own lawyer will advise you, comma, such an offence continues from day to day. Paragraph. My clients have no desire to see you publicly humiliated in Belston Magistrates' Court, comma, and have instructed me that they have always been willing to meet your grazing charges, stop, paragraph. Perhaps you will be good enough to let me know when and how the animals will be returned to my clients, stop, paragraph. Yours sincerely'.

I put down the mike and grinned at him. 'Does it really work? It hasn't been repealed or superseded?'

He grinned back. 'No', he said. 'Someone tried to argue in 1910 that it was obsolete, but the High Court said that it had never been repealed and unless Parliament repealed a statute it was available for use. Abraham Thornton's case from Sutton Coldfield, eighteen twenty-something, laid that down'.

'I hope he argues', I said. 'I'd love to put that smug swine into court'.

Alasdair took himself off and I turned to Mac's papers. His report confirmed what he had told me—that Sean McBride was a fit, healthy eighteen-year-old, with no signs of disease or injury. He showed the external symptoms of carbon monoxide poisoning and blood analysis confirmed this as the cause of death.

A bunch of photographs in a cardboard Central Midlands Police cover was attached to Mac's report. They also told me nothing new. There were external shots of the garage with the door closed and open, pictures of the car in the garage which showed the sexual detritus on the floor. There were pictures of the body slumped in the rear seat of the car and a photograph of the garage from above, which must have been taken from the flat block alongside the row of garages. It served to show where Charlie had pulled aside a loose sheet of the roofing so that he could look into the garage. None of it seemed to help.

Behind the photo album was a photocopy of a statement. It was from PC 279, Thompson, and said:

'On Tuesday 26th May I was on mobile patrol with PC 421, Port, when we were directed by the despatcher to a telephone call box in Wednesfield Road as the result of an emergency message sent from that box.

'On arrival we were met by a youth who I now know to be Charles NESBIT, aged eighteen, unemployed, of Flat 3, The Sandings, Shelley Place, Belston. He told us that he was concerned about a friend, Sean McBRIDE, who had been missing since the previous Friday evening. He had gone to a lock-up garage rented by McBRIDE and had looked in through an aperture in the roof. He said that he had seen McBRIDE lying dead or injured in a car that was in the garage.

'We made arrangements by radio for an ambulance to join us at the garage and we went there with NESBIT. The garage is the right-hand end one in a row that lies adjacent to the car-park of the Grenville House flat block. Waiting by the garage was a female youth who I now know to be Sylvia Mary WELLINGTON, aged sixteen, school student, of Old Leys, Blackberry Lane, Trosall, Salop.

She appeared very upset and I advised her to sit in the police car while we investigated.

'The youth NESBIT showed me how to gain access to the roof of the garages and pointed out where he had slid aside a loose area of roofing. I looked down into the garage through that aperture. I was able to see the front part of a red saloon car. From my viewpoint I was unable to determine the make or model and I could not see the registration number. The passenger's door was wide open and the front passenger seat had been removed. In the area previously occupied by the seat I could see a leg clothed in denim jeans and a left foot in a black trainer. It was evident that someone was lying in the back of the vehicle. I called McBRIDE's name several times loudly but I could not detect any movement nor hear any reply.

'At this juncture the ambulance arrived and a paramedic joined me on the roof. After assessing the situation he said that it would be necessary to force the door of the garage. We climbed down and with very little effort succeeded in breaking the lock of the garage and opening the door.

The paramedics entered the garage and later confirmed that they had found the dead body of a male youth in the rear seat of the car. It was their opinion that he had inhaled carbon monoxide and that his death might be suicide.

'The youth NESBIT identified the dead body as that of his friend, Sean McBRIDE. I informed Control by radio of our findings and waited until a Scenes of Crime Team arrived, when I took NESBIT and WELLINGTON to Belston Police Station. WELLINGTON was deeply upset, in fact nearly hysterical, and I judged it impossible to obtain a coherent statement from her. I arranged for her to be taken home by a female PC and I proceeded to take a witness statement from Charles NESBIT'.

The statement trailed off into formalities. I sat and thought. So, Sylvia Wellington had been with Nesbit when he discovered Sean. What on earth did that mean?

Charlie Nesbit's statement was behind the police officer's. He denied seeing Sean on the Friday night, saying that he last saw him on Thursday evening. He did not see Sean on Friday and did not call at his home because he knew that Sean was going away early on Saturday morning and thought he would be getting ready on Friday night. He was mystified when Mrs McBride had contacted him and said that Sean had never come home on Friday night. He had gone to Sean's garage, but found it locked and no sign that Sean was there. Later he had met Sylvia and they had discussed Sean's disappearance. She had said that the only place Sean could be was in the garage and that something must have happened to him. He agreed to go with her and check again, which was how he had come to climb on the roof and spot the body

Nothing helpful there, but another puzzle. If he'd already checked the garage and found nothing, what had convinced him to go back with Sylvia? Why hadn't he just told her it wasn't worth looking inside? Did she tell him something that led him to believe that Sean might be inside?

I glanced through the statement again. Charlie Nesbit was Sean's best mate. He was in lots of the photographs. He was with him up to the Thursday night. Surely the police had asked him if he could think of any reason why his mate had killed himself. If they had, there was no answer recorded in the statement—not a single word about breathalysers or headaches. If Sean really was worried about them, he never mentioned his worries to Charlie—or, alternatively, Charlie never mentioned them to the police.

I gave up and slid the folder into my briefcase, intending to let Sheila apply her tortuous intelligence to it. I needed to contact Sylvia Wellington's dad.

CHAPTER FOURTEEN

I was lucky. Wellington wasn't in Tokyo or Rio de Janeiro when I called; he was actually at his desk.

'Chris!' he exclaimed as he took the call, as though we are old mates. We're not—I'd met him three times at legal seminars about how to get more blood out of the same stone and how to charge for the same work three times and other useful legal skills. 'What gives me the pleasure?' he asked.

'We need to meet', I said. 'Soon'.

'You sound deathly urgent', he said. 'You've got a deal for me?'

'No', I said. 'I've got a warning for you. About your daughter. I need to see you'.

'My daughter?' he said, puzzled. 'You sound as if she's in some kind of trouble'.

'I hope I'm wrong', I said, 'but I think she may be in serious danger'.

He was still puzzled, and I didn't blame him. 'Serious danger? What about?'

'About Sean McBride', I said.

'But Sean McBride's dead. He committed suicide'.

'Maybe he didn't. There were three pals—Sean McBride, Charlie Nesbit and your Sylvia, right?'

'Right', he agreed.

'Sean's dead in what may not have been suicide. Now Charlie's dead in what may not have been suicide. I need to tell you about it and you need to listen'.

His voice ceased to be puzzled and became business-like. 'The quicker the better, it seems'. I heard pages riffle. 'As it happens, I'm free for lunch. Are you still in that delightful Victorian building down in the Square? What about the Jubilee Room at one? Yes? That's a date then'.

That was the easy part. The difficult part was going to be seeing how much he knew about Sylvia's relationship with Sean, what his attitude had been and how far he was prepared to talk about it. I was going to earn my lunch.

When I went over to the Victoria Hotel, I found him waiting for me in the Durbar Lounge. He was slightly older than me, say about forty. Tall, tanned, immaculately covered in an expensive dark blue suit. Smiling blue eyes looked out of the tan under a thick head of fair hair only just beginning to turn. His cufflinks must have cost more than my monthly Legal Aid cheque.

He shook me warmly by the hand and bought me a drink. While we drank the barman took our lunch order.

When we were seated over a table in the Jubilee Room he looked at me steadily.

'They say you're not a man who panics', he

remarked.

'I try not to', I said, 'but I get frightened and I'm frightened now. Where's your daughter?'

'She's at home, with my wife and our staff'.

'Good', I said. 'Tell them not to let her out of sight'.

'Are you going to tell me why?'

'Look', I began, 'How much do you know about Sylvia's friendship with Sean McBride?'

He smiled. 'I know they were what they would have called an item, if that's what you mean'.

'And did you approve?'

'No. Of course not. Don't get me wrong. There was nothing I could see wrong about young McBride. He was a skilled mechanic and I'm quite prepared to agree that a skilled mechanic is as good as a skilled lawyer, but most of the rest of the world doesn't. He wasn't exactly what my wife and I wanted for Sylvia, I'm sure you understand that'.

I nodded. 'Did you take any steps to stop them?'

He shook his head. 'Oh, no. I'm not that daft. I wasn't going to play the heavy father and have Sylvia pregnant and the pair of them running off to Gretna Green. I just let it ride. I was fairly certain that it would burn out in time and someone else would come along'.

'Did they break up before he died?' I asked.

'No', he said. 'As far as I can tell they'd been planning to go away that weekend, but something went wrong. She told us a tale about staying with a friend and she went off on the Saturday morning, but she came back, saying her friend was ill. Then she was buzzing about all weekend, coming and going, then she heard about his death and she broke up completely. We had a dreadful time with her for a few weeks. I sent her to friends in Florida, but she drove them crazy and, anyway, she had to come back for school. She's still not over it really'.

'So she never gave him the elbow?'

'Definitely not'.

'Did you know the boy at all?'

'I met him a number of times. In fact, he met Sylvia because I needed a mechanic urgently on a Sunday evening and someone recommended him. He came out to my place and he did a good job. That's when he first met Sylvia. I saw him a few times with her. He always seemed a reasonable, decent kind of lad'.

'You don't know anything about him suffering from headaches that worried him?'

He frowned. 'Nobody ever said anything about that to me. I don't think Sylvia knew about it. Her uncle's a doctor, she'd have bothered him about it. Why do you ask?'

'Because that's one of the reasons that the Coroner said "Suicide."'

'That man's too old for his job', he said. 'What was the other?'

101

'Would you believe a breathalyser charge?'

He grinned. 'People don't top themselves over breathalysers, do they? My clients don't'.

'My clients sign on till they get their licences back. I imagine yours hire chauffeurs'.

'Stop fighting the class war, Chris, and tell me about the danger to Sylvia'.

I told him—all of it. He grew more and more thoughtful and less interested in his food as the story went on. When I finished he poured us both more wine.

'You're right', he said. 'This thing stinks of something very peculiar. Even if it turns out to have been something between Sean and the Nesbit lad, I don't want Sylvia mixed up in it. She's had enough. I'm going to send her abroad again'.

I nodded. 'Good idea', I agreed, 'but there is one thing. If you're willing, I'd very much like to talk to her'.

He frowned. 'I don't know, Chris. I told you—she's had a very hard time with it. What good will it do, trying to make her go over it again?'

'It might do her a lot of good', I said. 'Survivors always feel guilty, don't they? She isn't just someone who survived the death of someone close, Tom, she was his sweetheart. She will be thinking that if anything was worrying him or frightening him or depressing him, she was the one person who should have known, who he would have talked to, who should have been able to make it right for him. But she didn't and he died. She must be carrying an appalling load of guilt. If I can even make her see that it might have been an accident, then that's got to relieve a lot of guilt, hasn't it?'

He stared at me for a while, then I could see him make his mind up. 'I'm not going to force her', he said, 'but you can try. It'll have to be soon. I really am going to get her abroad fast. I can't keep her on a lead and I want her out of the country until we know what this mess is really about. I'll talk to her and I'll come back to you as soon as I can'.

I couldn't ask for better. We finished eating and I let him take the bill.

CHAPTER FIFTEEN

'I thought it was a total waste of time, that meeting. I spent hours trying to convince Capstick that we needed his input at BDS to break the deadlock, but he wouldn't listen'.

I was listening to Con Mulvaney's account of the BDS strike. He was talking about the visit that he and Martin and Mohammed had made to the Union's National Secretary.

'Utter waste of time', he emphasised. 'All he kept saying was that we'd allowed the Union to get a bad reputation with BDS for wildcat walkouts and it was time we calmed down and talked to management civilly. I kept telling him that we'd tried that and tried it and they still kept up the undermanning and shoving people about from job to job'.

'So, how did it end?' I asked.

'Nowhere', he said. 'We just gave up and came away. It was the next day that things changed'.

'How?'

'Capstick rang me. That surprised me, for a start. He isn't a great one for ringing people out in the provinces, but I was even more surprised when I heard what he wanted to say. He said that he'd been turning the problem over with Fred Goatly, the Midland Secretary, and they'd decided to do something. He said that it was true that BDS had broken the Joint Agreement in the way they sacked Mohammed, and that he and Goatly had decided that Goatly would seek a meeting with BDS at which he would demand Mohammed's reinstatement and an end to the undermanning. Well, that stunned me for a start, but it got better. Capstick was going to serve notice on BDS of a strike ballot. He reckoned that an official legal warning might put BDS under enough pressure to make them see sense'.

'What's the Joint Agreement?' I asked.

'It's the National Joint Agreement on Working Practices. It's a set of rules drawn up between the Union and the Armament Manufacturers' Alliance years ago, back in the fifties'.

'And how had BDS breached it?'

'Well, there's a procedure laid down—step by step—in the Agreement, for sacking people. You can't just lose your rag and throw somebody out, not unless he's done something bloody awful, but refusing an order, that has to go by the Agreement, step by step. They never even started the procedure. They just threw him out because he talked back'.

'I'll need to see the latest version of the National Agreement', I said, 'the one in force when Mohammed was sacked'.

He peered into the battered briefcase on the chair alongside him and fished out a fat, orange-covered volume.

'That's it', he said. 'The 1992 edition, with the latest amendments. There's a marker in the Discipline and Dismissal section'.

I put the book into my own briefcase and looked over my notes.

'What did you think when Capstick changed his tack?'

'I thought he'd had an attack of common-sense, that's all. What we were trying to say to BDS was quite fair and he always should have backed us'.

'And what happened?'

'Well, a few days later Goatly came up from London . . .'

'He's based in London? I thought he was the Midland Secretary?'

'Well, he used to stay in Birmingham, but since Capstick's been ill, Goatly's been working a lot at Head Office, giving Capstick a hand. Everyone reckons that Capstick'll resign at the next Conference and recommend Goatly for National Secretary'.

'Would that be a good move?'

He shook his head. 'No', he said. 'Goatly's a company man. He's the kind of bloke who's got the Union a name as a company union. He'll do whatever they want. Like he did this time'.

'You were telling me', I said. 'He came up from London . . .'

'That's right. He came up and had a meeting with me and Jim and Mohammed and the other Shop Stewards, to make sure he'd got all of our side of the story. Then he had a meeting with BDS'.

'Who did he meet with?'

'The MD, Personnel and the Legal Officer'.

'Were you at that meeting?'

'No'.

'Why not?'

'Goatly said that it'd be better if he came in as a new broom, a fresh face on the problem. He said my history with the company might cause personality problems and stop the matter getting resolved'.

'Is that what you thought?'

'No. I didn't like the idea of him having a closed meeting with management, but that was the way he wanted it'.

'So he had one, and what happened?'

'Well, Brother Goatly came out of the meeting well pleased. According to him, everything was solved, it was all OK, it was back to the beginning and a fresh start and I don't know what'.

'But . . . ?'

'But, he'd carved it up with them, hadn't he? Management had agreed—unofficially and off the record—that they broke the rules when they sacked Mohammed, so he could have his job back and nothing would be held against him'.

'That sounds OK'.

'So it was, but there was another thing. We'd always wanted Mohammed reinstated without any loss, and by this time we'd been fooling about for a couple of weeks. There was a couple of weeks' pay to think about. So I asked Goatly what was to happen about that'.

'And what did he say?'

'He said he'd got the best deal he was going to get, that BDS wouldn't pay, they'd only take him back'.

'But that wasn't a full reinstatement', I said. 'If they didn't treat him as an employee during the period of absence, they were re-employing him, not reinstating him'.

He nodded. 'That's what I told Goatly. I

told him that Mohammed's pension situation, his promotion, all sorts of things could be affected if he didn't make them accept a full reinstatement with pay for the intervening period, but he wasn't going to have it. He just said that you can't have everything your own way, and that Mohammed might learn to keep his temper in future. And that was it—Goatly just buggered off back to London and left it like that'.

'And what did you do?'

'Well, we had a meeting of the Shop Stewards and they went up the wall when I told them what Goatly had done. Some of them were for a walkout, but I stopped that. I said we'd do it properly or not at all'.

'So, what did you do?'

'Well, it dawned on me that Capstick's notice of a strike ballot was still in place, so we went ahead. We held a strike ballot'.

'Was that legal?'

'You're the lawyer—you tell me'.

CHAPTER SIXTEEN

I was worried. In fact, I was very worried. I suspected that we had just found a large hole in any case that might be made for Con Mulvaney.

'Why did you do it?' I asked.

'Because I was furious with Goatly, that's why'.

'Fine, but did you realise that what you were doing might be illegal?'

'How was it illegal?' he challenged.

'Look', I said. 'Before Goatly met with BDS, Capstick had served the notice required by law that the branch was going to be balloted for a strike, yes?'

'Yes', he agreed impatiently.

'Then Goatly came to his compromise—on behalf of the Union'.

'He wasn't acting on behalf of the Union', said Mulvaney. 'He didn't do what we asked him to do. That was the whole point'.

'You're missing mine', I said. 'Goatly believed—or at least, he said he believed—that he'd got the best deal available, didn't he?'

'Right', said Mulvaney, 'but he never intended it to go to a strike ballot and he never really threatened them with it'.

'How do you know that?'

'Because he said so. He thought a strike would be destructive to the firm's interests and would only lose members' jobs'.

'So he accepted the compromise?'

'Right—and made a victim out of Mohammed'.

'But what was going to happen when Goatly reported back to Capstick in London? Surely, Goatly was going to say that he'd done the best deal that he could in all the circumstances?'

Mulvaney snorted. 'Well, of course he was. He wasn't going to tell Capstick that he'd got it all wrong—deliberately.'

'We can't challenge Goatly's honesty in the negotiations unless we can prove it. Can you?'

'Of course not! I wasn't bloody there, was I?'

'Right, but Capstick accepted Goatly's version of affairs and withdrew the strike notice? Yes?'

'Well, of course he did. That's why I went ahead. Sort of pre-emptive strike', and he grinned.

'It might have been if you'd had the right to issue a strike notice, but you had no right to go ahead, did you? The notice of no strike was issued from London on behalf of the Union nationally, in the proper form required by law. How could you—as a provincial Branch Secretary—go on without Head Office support?'

'I had to', he said. 'It's in the Union's rules'.

'Really?' I said.

'Yes', he said, and delved again into his dog-eared briefcase. He emerged with a battered blue book and began to thumb through it. Eventually he passed the open volume across to me.

'There', he said, pointing. 'After the bit about "Election of Branch Officers" there's a piece about "Duties of Branch Officers".

That's what I was going under'.

I read the passage aloud:

'Once elected, Branch Officers are subject in the first place to the wishes of the Membership of their Branch as expressed by a majority vote of a General Meeting of the Branch'.

'That's it!' he said, triumphantly. 'I had no other obligation but to the Branch Membership'.

'Not according to your Rules', I agreed, 'but it isn't that easy. The Tribunal will say that there's nothing illegal in these Rules, but they're subject to statute law and that, I suspect, says differently'.

He stared at me. 'I had to do what the Members wanted', he said.

'Not if the law of England says differently', I said. 'Statute law takes precedence over anybody's rules. I think we've got a problem. However, I'll check it out. In the meantime, what happened about the ballot?'

'I reported to a General Meeting of the Branch on Goatly's cop out and that was it—the ballot was nearly one hundred per cent for strike action'.

'And it was a proper ballot? Not one of your old-fashioned showing of hands on the works car-park jobs?'

'Do me a favour!' he said. 'It was absolutely straight. One member, one ballot paper. Secret voting. All shipshape'.

111

'And then what?'

'Then I issued due notice to BDS that we had voted to strike'.

'Which you had no right to do?'

'Of course I did'. He pointed at the Rules again. 'I had an obligation to do it once the Branch had voted, didn't I?'

'Assuming', I said, 'that the notice of the ballot was legal and that the ballot was legal and that the vote was properly conducted, somebody had an obligation to inform BDS, but shouldn't it have been Capstick, not you?'

'Somebody had to do it on the Unions behalf. Why shouldn't it have been me?'

'You're dodging, Con. You'd already taken on the function of your National Secretary when you went ahead with the ballot. Weren't you doing the same again when you issued the strike notice to BDS?'

'I had an obligation to the Branch', he repeated doggedly.

'OK, OK. So you issued notice of the vote to BDS and the strike went ahead, yes?'

'Right'.

'And on the first day of the strike, you and Martin got into a fight with your boss, right?'

'No', he said. 'Not right. It was self-defence'.

I looked at my watch. 'There's no time to deal with it now', I said. 'You'll have to come back again, I'm afraid'.

'Don't worry about it', he said. 'I've got nothing else to do'.

CHAPTER SEVENTEEN

I was still worrying about the hole in Mulvaney's story as I walked home. Mohammed had been sacked for disobeying an order. I thought I could win that argument. Jim Martin had been sacked for assaulting the boss. He and Mulvaney assured me that they had independent witnesses to say it was self-defence, so I might win that one. Mulvaney was sacked for the assault also, but principally for calling an illegal strike, and now it looked as if that was exactly what he had done. Ah well—you can't win them all.

The day had turned cold and grey. When I got home Sheila was already in the kitchen.

'Hi!' she said, without looking round. 'It was cold, so I thought you might like something hot'.

I pinched her backside gently. 'As soon as I walked into the kitchen I fancied something hot. Why don't we forget dinner, get swiftly drunk and go to bed?'

'Huh', she snorted. 'What's wrong with the front room carpet these days?'

'That's for winter when the curtains are drawn', I said. 'I don't want to cause heart attacks on the top of a double decker bus'.

'There aren't any buses along this road', she pointed out. 'Truth is, you're just a stuffy old pom, afraid of what the neighbours think'.

'Truth is', I said, 'that we have experience of chilly weather hereabouts, and the best place is in bed'.

She turned from the worktop and kissed me. 'In South Australia we don't have cold weather', she said. 'There are parts where it's 125 degrees in midsummer'.

'Sure', I agreed. 'The parts where nobody lives. Anyway, why have you taken over my turn to cook?'

'Told you. I thought you'd fancy something warm after a hard day at the office'.

'What you really mean is that either Mac or John Parry has wheedled a free meal out of us and they both prefer your cooking'.

'Well, yair, that as well. John rang and said he'd got some info about the McBride affair'.

'I have been wrestling, for much of this afternoon, with the fact that I'm probably going to lose Con Mulvaney's case, and you want me to waste my evening talking to John Parry about a case that I can't do anything about anyway?'

'Hoy!' she said, 'Go and pour yourself a drink and keep out from underfoot till John gets here. After which you can be rude to him if you like'.

So I withdrew.

Parry turned up with a bottle of Talisker in tow and we settled to eat. Sheila's work was quite sufficient to stop us talking shop until we got to the coffee and whisky stage.

'I have a few bits of information about Charlie Nesbit', the big Welshman said, 'not to mention a bit about Sean McBride'.

'He thinks it's none of his business', said Sheila. 'He's more interested in his old strike case'.

John looked from one to another of us. 'Have you kiddies been scrapping again? Shall I go out and come in again, or shall I just kiss the hostess and slink away into the night?'

'If it'll stop you mauling my fiancée, I'll listen to what you've got to say about Nesbit and McBride'.

He nodded. 'Did you know that Kath McBride's gaff was burgled a few days before Sean died?'

'What?' I ejaculated. 'I've not heard that!'

'It's true, though, boyo. She says that they were all out at the pictures one evening and when they got back the glass in the back door had been smashed, the door opened and someone had been in'.

'Was anything taken?'

'Well now, that's the peculiar bit, isn't it? Most of the house only showed odd little indications that someone had been there—you know, things out of their usual place, but Sean's room had been gone over in some detail. Nevertheless, as far as Kath knows, nothing was missing'.

'That's pretty bloody odd', said Sheila. 'Did

she report it?'

John shook his head. 'No. Kath took the view that we don't take any notice of burglaries in general on that estate and we certainly wouldn't want to be bothered by a burglar who didn't steal anything, and she's probably right'.

'What do you think they—he—she—was after? Any idea?'

'Well, they left Sean's camera and his music gear. They left the telly and the video in the sitting room. It certainly wasn't your average estate burglar. But what they really wanted, I don't know. Sean wasn't into drugs, so far as the Drug Squad knows, he wasn't into thieving, and he kept his cash in a bank account. That leaves something personal'.

'Something personal?' Sheila queried.

'Yes. Perhaps something that he'd had from someone else that they wanted to get back'.

'Why not ask?' I said.

'Because, presumably, he wouldn't hand it over'.

'What on earth are we talking about here? Are you saying he was into blackmail?'

'No, no', he said. 'It's just that all the obvious reasons for burglary are out, so it's got to be something peculiar, and it certainly seems that someone was looking for something they expected to be in Sean's room. So—he may have had something of somebody else's. That's my thinking'.

'Doesn't take you very far, does it?' said Sheila.

'Well, no', he agreed. 'But it helps to confirm the impression that there was something going on around young McBride that we haven't discovered yet'.

'You sure it wasn't drugs?' asked Sheila.

'The usual answer that we heavy-footed plods jump to when serious malarkey breaks out amongst youngsters is drugs, but I promise you, no one—absolutely no one—puts Sean down as into drugs—neither using nor selling'.

'What about the girlfriend?'

'Sylvia Wellington? A puff of pot at parties, maybe. Nothing else. Tom Wellington would have killed her if he even dreamed of anything else. Again—nothing from the Drug Squad'.

'Does the Drug Squad know every drug user in town?' I asked.

'No', he said, 'but they soon get to know the serious ones and any who deal, and that wasn't McBride or Sylvia Wellington'.

'So that takes us nowhere', remarked Sheila.

'It is', said John, 'more information, and more information is always good news to a policeman'.

'Huh!' she said, 'Except when you haven't got the least idea what it means'.

'I have demonstrated to you', he said, 'that at least we know what it doesn't mean, which is nearly as good. Kindly remember Sherlock Holmes and the dog that didn't bark. Value of negative evidence and all that'.

'Smarmy and cunning but no cigar', she announced.

'Wait', he said, 'until I tell you about Nesbit'.

'What about Nesbit?' I said.

'Doc's been at him and given me the benefit of his observations. Firstly, I was right about the small abrasion on his knee and the tear in his jeans. Doc says the injury was from hitting the floorboard on the move, and that it happened very shortly before death or it would have bled a lot more. He also says that someone probably gripped Charlie's neck with a left hand, very forcefully'.

'So, what do you think happened?' I asked.

'Just as I speculated before', he said, smugly. 'Someone lay in wait in the little hallway by the bathroom. When Nesbit came back from the pub and headed straight for the loo, that someone stepped out behind him, took him by the neck with his left hand, forced him down against the bath and shot him through the right side of his head'.

'Possible', I said, 'but it's a bit slender. Suppose he got slewed at the pub, came over all drunkenly remorseful about Sean's death, decided to end it all, went home, took his little pistol, went into the bathroom and slumped drunkenly to his knees by the bath, thereby scraping his knee on the floor, then shot himself?'

'I know', John said. 'I'm not happy with it. I need more. There's the marks on his neck, but they could have been made anytime really'.

'They weren't', announced Sheila. 'He was murdered'.

'Says who?' I demanded.

'Says me, cobber'. She got up and left the room, returning with a handful of Polaroid photos. 'You were there', she said to John. 'Remember the guitar and banjo in the front room?'

'Yes', he said, slowly and perplexed.

'Notice anything about them?' Sheila asked.

He shook his head. 'Not much', he said. 'There was a six-string acoustic guitar and a four-string tenor banjo. That's all. Nothing surprising, Nesbit had played with Irish groups since he was a kid'.

'And I thought the Welsh were musical', she said. She riffled through the Polaroids and dropped one on the table. 'Look at the strings', she commanded.

John and I both looked. After a moment John said, 'When was this taken?'

'Ah, yes, well', I began, 'While we were waiting for you to arrive, I took the opportunity to take a few reference shots'.

He stared at me, blankly. 'As an all-too-frequent discoverer of dead bodies', he said, heavily, 'you might be expected to know the rules, mightn't you? You call the police and leave the scene strictly alone'.

'I promise you', I said, 'I never smoked, breathed, spat, sweated or even thought while I was in that room. I just felt that if I had pictures of my own it would save me asking you to wangle me copies of the official ones when it wasn't even my case'.

'Very thoughtful of you', he said. 'Now then, what's with these instruments?'

'The strings', Sheila said. 'Look at them'.

He looked again. 'I was right', he said. 'A six-string acoustic guitar and a four-string banjo. So what?'

She snorted impatiently 'What a pair of galahs!' she said and got up again to leave the room.

She came back with her guitar and sat with it across her knee, as though she was going to play.

'Do you know "Isle of Capri"?' John asked. 'My mother was very fond of that'.

Sheila snorted again. 'Observe', she commanded. 'Here I have a bog standard six-string guitar. Note that the so-called "top" string—the thinnest, highest-pitched one—is at the bottom of the array when the instrument is in playing position. Conversely, the so-called "bottom" string—the thickest, lowest note—is at the top of the array'.

"All very simple and lucid', John remarked.

She shot him an eloquent scowl. 'Now, watch closely, because there'll be questions', she continued, lifting the instrument and holding it upright. 'See—the bass string is to your left and the treble to your right. Right?'

We nodded.

'Now look at the piccy, you galahs!'

We did, and both saw it simultaneously. 'They're back to front!' exclaimed John. 'Back-strung!' I said.

'Precisely Watson', she said. 'Charlie Nesbit was left-handed. If he'd shot himself, the entry wound would have been on the left side and the pistol would have fallen in the bath'.

She glared at us both, triumphantly.

'You're not just a pretty face and a funny accent, are you?' said John. 'You've solved my problem, you've made my case. Let me give you a big sloppy kiss'.

'No, ta. Just fill the whisky glass', she said.

We refilled and John and I toasted her.

'Just one other little thing', said John, after a long swallow. 'You don't happen to be able to prove who did it and why, do you?'

CHAPTER EIGHTEEN

We laughed—the way you do when you've had a drink and you think you're doing well. The trouble with drink is that it won't cheer you up—it'll only make you feel like you do already but more so, if you know what I mean. A few drinks later the delight at Sheila's observation had dissolved and we were sitting round silently sipping and looking at the photographs and the drink was making us feel more so—more confused and puzzled.

'I suppose', John said glumly, 'that you really don't have any other amazing insights, Sheila?' and this time it wasn't a joke.

She shook her head. 'Not a skerrik'.

'I'd even take one of those if I knew what it was', he said. 'All I keep thinking about is the money'.

'What money?' Sheila and I asked in unison.

The big Welshman looked surprised. 'Haven't I told you about the money? The money in Nesbit's bank account?'

'I'm surprised he had a bank account', remarked Sheila.

'You almost have to have to get paid your dole nowadays', I said. 'Tell us about the money, John'.

'Well', he said, 'we always look for accounts as a matter of course. Charlie Nesbit had a building society cash card in his flat, and we checked it out. We thought there'd only be the remains of his dole in the account, but there was just over a thousand'.

Sheila and I gaped. 'How was the thousand accumulated?' I asked.

'One payment of a round grand', said John, 'paid in the Saturday morning after Sean McBride died, in cash. What do you make of that?'

Sheila frowned. 'Let me get this straight', she said. 'Sean disappears on a Friday evening—possibly in company with Charlie—and dies sometime that night, by accident or suicide. Then Charlie finds the body, but before Charlie has found the body—when no one knows that Sean is dead—someone plonks a grand into Charlie's account, right?'

'Right', we said.

'Then Charlie killed Sean', she announced.

'Thank you, Sherlock', I said. 'It doesn't work'.

'Oh yair?' she challenged. 'Someone breaks into Sean's pad and doesn't—apparently—find anything. So he commission's Charlie to kill Sean. Sean does it, reports to his employer and the money is paid in to his account. Then the employer stiffs Charlie to tie up a loose end'.

'Fine', I said, 'but, firstly, if Charlie killed Sean why did he find the body? Secondly, how did Charlie kill Sean? Sean died of carbon monoxide poisoning. Thirdly, if the employer is prepared to put a bullet in Charlie, why didn't he see to Sean himself, instead of wasting a grand on Charlie?'

She frowned again. John sprawled back in his chair and looked at her, watching her grapple with my questions. 'He's right', he said, after a while. 'It won't work that way. You can make Sean's death an accident, not a suicide, but you can't make it a murder—by Charlie or anyone else. Like Chris says, he died of monoxide poisoning. You can't murder someone that way unless they're already unconscious. There's nothing to suggest that Sean was artificially unconscious. It looks like he had his wicked will of Sylvia, she went off and left him and he sat in the car and was silly enough to leave the engine running,'.

'He wouldn't have done that', Sheila said. 'He was a mechanic'.

'That's what happened', John said.

'So you think Charlie's death is a coincidence?' she demanded.

'Charlie's death, as you have brilliantly pointed out', he said, 'was a murder, not an accident or a suicide'.

'And you think it's pure coincidence that Charlie takes Sean away from home on the night Sean died, that he gets paid a load of money by persons unknown for reasons unknown, that he finds Sean's body, that he haunts Kath with his tape on the phone, and then he just happens to get murdered himself? Come on, John Parry, there's coincidences enough there to choke a stockman's dog, and I thought you didn't like coincidences!'

'I don't', he agreed. 'I thought that Sean and Charlie both committing suicide was a bit iffy, though people do top themselves because someone else has, but you got rid of that coincidence for me, didn't you? Now I've got a murder to solve—the murder of Charlie Nesbit. In the course of looking into that, I shall have to consider whether he took Sean away from home, why he was paid a grand on the following morning, and why he found the body and made those creepy phone calls, but that doesn't mean I think Sean was murdered. At present I think that Sean died by accident and that Charlie was up to something that had nothing to do with Sean and has ended up killed because of it'.

Sheila merely snorted and topped up her drink. I sat and pondered, to no point at all. John was right—the connection between the two deaths was that Charlie apparently took Sean away from his home on the night that he died and that he found the body, but that might be innocent and might simply arise out of them being pals. Sean might well have died by accident, but murder seemed impossible.

We chewed it round some more, but we got no further. Sheila wanted to believe in two murders, I sympathised with her and half-believed her and John wasn't having any. Dead end.

CHAPTER NINETEEN

Dennis Maiden came back fighting in the next morning's mail, or at least his solicitor did. A letter from an expensive Birmingham firm announced that:

'Mr Maiden is amused by your attempt to use the Distress Act against him, the more so since we have advised him that the Act is several centuries old and has not been used since 1910. In the circumstances he instructs us that he is still awaiting payment of his account in this matter and that, if the bill is not paid very shortly, he will feel obliged to dispose of the animals'.

After the previous day's problems and frustrations I was in an aggressive mood. I rang up the writer of the letter and introduced myself.

'A nice try', he complimented me, 'but you didn't really think it would work, did you. The Act's dead. It doesn't appear in the literature since 1910'.

'True', I agreed, 'but have you, by any chance, read the 1910 case?'

Of course he hadn't. Lawyers have almost never read the cases they quote glibly.

'As a matter of fact, no', he admitted. 'Is it relevant?'

'Very much so', I said. 'As far back as 1910, someone tried to get out of a Distress Act action by claiming that the Act was so old it was no longer law. It didn't work. The Court reminded them that an Act of Parliament has to be specifically repealed before it ceases to be law. I'm sure you remember Ashcroft—v—Thornton—after all, it was a Midlands case—when that principal was established'.

'Well, yes', he said, slowly, and I could almost hear the cogs of his brain racing, 'but it really doesn't work, does it?'

'Why not?' I demanded.

'Because if your client had put a car into my client's garage and refused to pay for the repairs, my client could seize the car against the debt, and if the debt wasn't paid he could dispose of it. That's the law as it is today, isn't it?'

'True, but the beauty of the Distress Act is that it doesn't deal with cars and garages. It deals with horses and cattle, and it says that you can seize them for debt, but you can't take them more than three miles or across a county boundary'.

'Ah!' he said, snatching at the weak point in my argument. 'How can you prove that my client has breached the Act by crossing a county boundary or taking the animals more than three miles? You have no proof of that!'

Nor did I. It was merely reasonable supposition that Maiden had the animals at his country gaff.

'Come on!' I said, bluffing like crazy. 'We both know where your client has got the ponies, and we both know that you can't get them there without crossing a county line—two if you go some ways—and it's certainly a lot more than three miles'.

'Well, yes', he agreed. 'But how did you know where they were?'

'I didn't', I said. 'You've just confirmed a reasonable suspicion, for which I thank you, though I doubt if Maiden will'.

There was a goodish pause, while he considered the prospects of admitting to Dennis Maiden that he'd just blown the case and exposed Maiden to prosecution under a sixteenth century cattle-rustling statute.

'I suppose', he said at last, 'that I can advise Mr Maiden, in the interest of goodwill, to return the animals and accept only the grazing fees due to him'.

'Very wise', I said. 'I'm most grateful for your help. Let me know when my clients can have their ponies back'.

That cheered me up quite a bit, so much so that I felt able to tackle the gap in Con Mulvaney's case. I was deep in that when the phone rang again.

'Mr Tyroll', said the unmistakable tones of Dennis Maiden. 'I've just had my solicitor onto me. He tells me that this ridiculous piece of law you've dug up actually works'.

'That's not the view he put to me', I said. 'He told me that it was out of date and dead'.

'Well, you've changed his mind, you smart bugger. He says that I've got to give the ponies back'.

'That would be sensible', I said. 'In return for which, my clients will meet that part of your bill that relates to grazing fees'.

'Right', he said. 'Tell your blokes to ring my

Security Manager at my office. He'll arrange for them to get the animals back'.

'Thank you', I said, 'Nice dealing with you, Mr Maiden'.

'Ay', he said, 'Nice dealing with you too, bloody smart alec', and he chuckled before putting the phone down.

I rang Samson and passed on the good news, then dictated my bill. All in all, I felt quite pleased with myself. It's always a good feeling to win a case, and putting Maiden's nose out of joint pleased me especially.

I didn't know then that someone would end up dead because of it.

CHAPTER TWENTY

Mrs Johnstone looked older than when I last saw her, which wasn't surprising. It must have been about five years, and she was well into her seventies by now. She had been one of my early clients when I first began my own practice. She'd had a neighbour dispute and a small accident claim against the Corporation.

Now she wanted me to find out if she was divorced.

'Well, aren't you sure?' I asked, puzzled.

She shook her head. 'Not really Mr Tyroll', she said. 'You see, when we split up he said he would divorce me, but I don't know that he ever did'.

'But you'd have heard from the Court, or his solicitor', I objected.

'I never did', she said, 'and that's what worries me. He went back to Scotland and said that he'd divorce me, but I never heard'.

'And when was this?' I asked.

'Oh, it would be about twenty-five years ago', she said. 'That's it, about the time of Her Majesty's Jubilee'.

'And you've never enquired before?'

She shook her head. 'You see, it's never mattered before'.

I paused, looking to express myself carefully and keep my face straight. 'You're not', I said, 'thinking of marrying again?'

She laughed. 'Oh, Good Heavens no!' she exclaimed. 'It's my money, you see'.

'Your money?'

'That's right. I've got a little bit—well, quite a bit—put away, and there's my house'.

I recalled drafting her will. 'If I remember correctly, that all goes to your sister and her family'.

She smiled. 'That's what I want', she confirmed, 'but I don't want him to have any claim'.

'When did you last see your husband?' I asked.

'Twenty-five years ago. He went back to Scotland to work, and he said that he was going to divorce me, but I never heard from him again'.

'He could be dead', I suggested.

'That would be convenient', she said evenly.

I was evidently missing something here. 'Can you tell me why it's important now?' I asked.

'I've got to go into hospital, Mr Tyroll', she said. 'Sometime this autumn they said. Now, they say it will be alright, that there's nothing to worry about, but you do, don't you. Well, maybe not you, you're young, but at my age you can't go into hospital and be sure of coming out again, so the thing is, if anything happens to me I don't want Jamie to have any claim against my money or the house'.

Now I understood. 'He probably wouldn't have, anyway', I said, 'and if you haven't heard of him or from him in a quarter of a century, he probably doesn't know anything about you. How would he know if you died?'

'I know it's a very remote chance, Mr Tyroll, but I don't want there to be any possibility of that man having anything of mine. Can't you find out for me if I've been divorced?'

I know nothing at all about English matrimonial law and less than that about Scottish, but she was a long-standing client and she was looking at me expectantly as though I had a copy of her divorce decree in my drawer.

'Very well, Mrs Johnstone', I said. 'Where was your husband living in Scotland?'

'Aberdeen', she said. 'And he was doing

something connected with the oil-rigs, not on one but something to do with them'.

'And you don't have an address?'

She shook her head. 'Oh no. I never heard from him after he went up there'.

I collected a few more vague recollections from her, told her that I'd do my best, saw her out, and sat down and sighed.

The phone rang. It was Tom Wellington. 'Can you come over to my place tonight?' he asked. 'I'm sending Sylvia abroad tomorrow, so it'll be your last chance to talk to her'.

'Sure', I said. 'Look, I'm grateful for this, Tom. It can't be easy'.

'It wasn't', he said, tersely. 'Her mother doesn't agree. Luckily Sylvia thinks it might be a good idea, but mind how you go with her, Chris. I've seen you in court'.

'Come on, Tom. This is different. Anyway, I was going to ask if I could bring Sheila. Another woman might put Sylvia more at ease and Sheila gets along well with most people'.

'Good idea'. he said. 'See you both about eight, then?'

'Right'.

I knew where Tom's place is, though I'd never been honoured with an invitation before. Sheila was making bad jokes about seeing how a real Pommy lawyer lives when we came to the hill brow above the Wellington home. She pulled in and we scanned the landscape.

In the summer evening the valley below us looked delightful, all trees and meadows, but I saw no sign of a house.

'There it is', said Sheila, and pointed.

I looked in that direction and saw what I took to be a medium-sized light industrial plant nestling behind a grove of trees. It looked as if it turned out electric clocks or inflatable teddy bears.

'Can't be', I said.

'Nothing else in sight', she said, and started the car.

We followed the road into the valley; coming at last to a sign for Tom's place. The long drive led us through the grove of trees and around a wide lawn to the front of the building we had seen. It looked no better in close up, and I guessed that anyone without Tom's money and clout would never have got it past a Planning Officer.

As we pulled up, Tom emerged from the wide, glazed front door and raised a hand to us. After handshakes he led us inside and we began to see that, despite the industrial exterior, the interior was sumptuous.

The hall in which we paused was floored with parquet, ornamented with a few rich rugs. The rear wall was all glass and revealed that the house was built Roman villa style, in a square around an inner courtyard. Through the glass we could see a large garden, where several paths wandered through artfully designed rockery, shrubbery and flowers towards a wide lily pool with a small fountain. The roofline was low enough to allow the evening sun to light the garden for a while yet. I was frankly envious.

'No swimming pool, Tom?' I said.

He gestured to the right. 'Over there', he said. 'Indoors. Outdoor jobs are a waste of money in this climate'.

I saw that the right wing of the house was roofed in shatterproof glass where it covered the indoor pool, and realised that I had wasted my feeble joke.

Tom led us through to a drawing room, expensively furnished and again with a rear wall of sliding glass doors giving access to the central garden. We sat and he organised drinks.

'How are you planning to do this?' he asked, once we all had a glass in hand.

'I told you that my wife was pretty unhappy about it. She thinks it'll upset Sylvia all over again, so she's gone to a meeting so she can blame it all on me'.

'The last thing I want to do, Tom, is upset Sylvia any more', I said. 'I want to tell her that we're virtually certain that Sean didn't commit suicide. Surely, that's got to be good news for her?'

He nodded. 'Fair enough', he said, 'But what about this other suicide? What's his name—Nesbit?'

'She knows about that?'

'It's been in the papers', he said. 'It doesn't seem to have affected her, but she knew him as well'.

'Well', I said, 'one thing I can tell you, which hasn't reached the press yet, is that Charlie Nesbit didn't commit suicide. He was murdered'.

'Murdered!' he exclaimed. 'Why on earth would someone murder a feckless little runt like Nesbit?'

'We don't know', I said, 'but I can assure you that it was murder'.

His eyes narrowed. 'You're not saying, are you, that Sean was murdered?'

'No', I said. 'It seems most likely that Sean's death was an unlucky accident, but Charlie was definitely murdered'.

'You know', he said, thoughtfully, 'Sylvia said that once, that she thought Sean was murdered. She was very upset at the time, rambling about how he wouldn't have committed suicide and it couldn't be an accident'.

'Did she give any reason why she thought that?' asked Sheila.

He shook his head. 'No, she was just sounding off. I thought she was just desperate to reject the idea that he'd committed suicide'.

'Then anything we can tell her will be good news', I said. He nodded. 'So, how are you going to do it?'

'I'm going to tell her exactly what we've discovered, that it was most probably an accident, but it certainly wasn't suicide. Hopefully, after that, she may be willing to talk to us a bit and help us with a few answers'.

'Right', he said, and uncoiled himself from his chair. 'I'll fetch Sylvia'.

He was gone only briefly, returning with his daughter. She was no longer the vivacious little beauty who had graced Sean's snapshots. The long black hair that had bounced and whirled about her smiling features in his pictures now hung lifelessly round her pale face, and her eyes were big pools of darkness with shadows below.

She walked listlessly to a chair and sat silently while Tom introduced us.

'Chris and Sheila just want to tell you about the things they've found about Sean', he said. 'I think you'll want to hear what they've got to say, and maybe you can help them. It's for Mrs McBride's sake, really, and yours. You'd want to help Sean's mother, wouldn't you? You always said how you liked her'.

The silent girl nodded without looking up.

'I don't think you'll want me listening in', he went on, 'but I'll be just out in the garden, not far away if you want me'.

He nodded to us and let himself out into the courtyard, standing for a moment and looking back to us, then strolling away along one of the paths.

There was a silence after he left. Sylvia sat with her hands on her knees, one hand clutching a brightly coloured packet. At last she looked up and spoke. 'He didn't commit suicide, did he, Mr Tyroll?' she said, in a small voice. Her big, dead eyes swung from my face to Sheila's. 'Tell me he didn't. He couldn't have done'.

CHAPTER TWENTY-ONE

'Why couldn't he have done?' Sheila asked gently.

'Because—because he was happy. Everything was alright. We were going away the next morning'.

'Sylvia', I said, 'at the Inquest it was said that he was about to be in court for a breathalyser. Didn't that worry him?'

She shook her head. 'No', she said, emphatically 'He knew he'd lose his licence, but that didn't worry him much. Most of the time he walked, anyway, and there were plenty of people to give him lifts. That was why we were going away in the morning. He said that, since he was going to lose his licence, we'd better take our last chance to have a weekend away together'.

'Were you going to a friend's?' I asked.

'No', she said. 'I told my parents that I was

going alone to stay with a girlfriend, but really Sean and I were going for a weekend in a hotel'.

'Do your parents know now?' Sheila asked.

'I think Daddy suspects something like that, but they've never asked. You won't tell them, will you?'

'Of course not', I said. 'Tell me, do you know anything about Sean suffering from headaches?'

She shook her head emphatically. 'No', she said. 'There was nothing wrong with him. He was a joke in our crowd, because when everyone else had colds and 'flu he never seemed to catch it. All that at the Inquest was lies. He never had headaches'.

'The Inquest was told that his friends said he had headaches. Do you know who that was?' Sheila asked.

'I asked all our lot', the girl said. 'Most of them weren't even asked about him, and none of them said he had headaches because he didn't'.

Sheila looked at me with a wondering grimace. Sylvia said, 'He didn't commit suicide, Mr Tyroll. He couldn't have done, he wouldn't have done. What happened to him?'

'We don't believe it was suicide', I said, 'nor does the pathologist who did the post mortem, Dr Macintyre. He thinks that it was most likely some kind of accident'.

'What kind?' Sylvia asked, staring at me

with her big, dark eyes.

'We don't know', I said, carefully. 'How often was Sean in that garage?'

'He was there all the time when he wasn't with me. I used to tell him he fancied the car more than me'.

'So he knew the garage and he must have been aware of the danger from exhaust fumes—he was a mechanic', said Sheila.

'Is that what you think happened?' Sylvia asked.

'It might have done', I said. 'What do you remember about the last time you saw him? How did you come to be together at the garage?'

'Well', she began, 'we weren't going to see each other that evening, originally. We were going to meet up the next morning and go away for our weekend. That night my mother was dragging Daddy and I to one of her dos, but it was called off, so I wanted to see Sean. No one was answering the phone at his home, so I called Charlie Nesbit and asked him if he'd find Sean and tell him that I'd see him at the garage'.

'Did you have a key?' I asked.

'No', she said. 'I just used to hang about the yard by the garages if I got there first. That's what I did that night. Then Sean came and we went in and got in the car'. Her voice trailed away, and for the first time her face showed a little colour.

'We don't need to know what you did, Sylvie', Sheila assured her. 'What sort of a mood was Sean in?'

'He was up, pleased to see me. He hadn't expected to see me that night till he got my message from Charlie'.

'And you didn't have any kind of disagreement?' I asked.

'No, no, no', she said. 'We were fine—everything was alright, we were looking forward to a weekend together'.

'What did you talk about?' I said.

'Where we were going for the weekend, what we'd do, that kind of thing. Nothing special'.

'What time did you leave?' Sheila said.

'I had to be home by eleven', Sylvia replied. 'So I left Sean about half past ten, near enough'.

'And where was Sean when you left him?' I asked.

'He was sitting in the back seat of the car. The front seat was out on the floor. He took it out so that we could be more comfortable on the back seat'. She coloured up again. 'He was going to put it back in, ready for the morning'.

'Did you close the door behind you?' Sheila asked.

'Yes. It wasn't open very far. I ducked underneath it and pulled it down, shut'.

'Why was that?' I asked.

'Sean always kept it pulled down and locked

when he was working in there. He said there were some strange people in the flats by the garages and he didn't want them bothering him. He'd got really good tools in there as well'.

'How did the door lock?' Sheila said.

'It was automatic. Once you pulled it right down into place the lock operated and you could only open it with a key'.

'But Sean had a key and you didn't?'

'That's right'.

'Do you know how the garage was ventilated?' I asked. 'When Sean worked in there with the door shut, how did air get in?'

'He'd lifted one of the panels in the roof and pushed it over a bit. When it rained the water used to come in, but it was by the side. It never got on the car or anything. That was how Charlie could see in when we went there'.

'And the next morning he didn't show up to pick you up?' I said.

She nodded. 'That's right. He was supposed to pick me up at the Belston Lane roundabout, but he didn't turn up'.

'What did you do?' asked Sheila.

'Well, when it got late I tried to ring Charlie—I rang Sean before, but there was no answer and I thought he was on the way to pick me up—but Charlie wasn't answering. Then I rang Penny—she's the friend I was supposed to be going to see and we had to sort out a story and then I went home'.

'What did you think had happened, Sylvie?' Sheila asked.

The girl twisted her head. 'I don't know! I didn't know! I couldn't think what had happened'.

'You didn't think he might have changed his mind?' I asked.

'No!' she said, 'No! Sean wasn't like that. If he said a thing, he'd do it. If he hadn't wanted to go with me, he'd have said so'.

'Did you think he might have dropped you?' Sheila asked quietly.

Sylvia stared at her. 'No!' she repeated, 'No! He absolutely wouldn't have done that. Anyway, he wasn't going to drop me. He kept asking me to marry him'.

'You're too young', I said.

'I know that', she said. 'I kept telling him that, but he kept on, saying it would be a long engagement, till I was old enough. It was a sort of joke between us, but Sean meant it, really. He'd said it once or twice before, but after the party he kept on about it'.

'What party?' said Sheila.

'We went to a party', Sylvia said. 'It was Penny's brother's engagement party. It was a really good time'. Her face screwed up and I thought the tears were going to break at last, but she recovered herself after a moment. 'It was at the Royal Oak. It was the week before . . . before Sean died'.

She half stood and thrust the paper packet

she had been holding at Sheila. 'There's some photos', she said. 'Sean took them and I got them processed. I never had a chance to give them to him. I expect Kath would like them. He's in two of them'.

Sheila took the packet and slipped it into her capacious shoulder-bag. 'What happened after the Saturday, Sylvie?' she asked.

'Kath rang me on the Saturday and said that he'd gone out with Charlie on Friday night and hadn't come home. I didn't tell her about Friday night and I didn't tell her about planning to go away with him on Saturday. He'd just told her that he was going to a mate's up north. I told her I hadn't seen him at all'.

Now the tears did come. She lowered her head and they poured down her face while her hands twisted in her lap, without even the packet of photos to occupy them.

At last she thrust her head up. 'Do you think that made any difference?' she asked, plaintively. 'If I'd told Kath about him being at the garage on Friday night—would that have made any difference?'

'If you mean, would it have saved Sean, Sylvie, the answer's no', Sheila said. 'He died pretty quickly, late on Friday night according to Doc Macintyre. Nothing you said did any harm'.

The girl's shoulders drooped with relief. Sheila passed a tissue and she wiped her eyes.

'I'm sorry', she said, 'but I was so afraid that

I'd caused it'.

She took a breath and carried on. 'After I talked to Kath I didn't know what to think. I'd been worried when Sean never turned up to pick me up, but I couldn't think why he hadn't gone home on Friday night. I tried to call Charlie, but I couldn't get hold of him. I kept trying him all through Sunday and Monday, but there was no answer. Then I got hold of him on Tuesday morning. He said that Kath had been on to him and been looking all over the place for Sean. When I told him about Saturday morning, he said that must mean that Sean had vanished on Friday night, and he thought we ought to check out the garage'.

'Did he say why? To check out the garage?' I interrupted.

'Not really, he just said that it was the last place either of us had seen him, so we'd better start there'.

'And, if he wasn't there, where was Charlie going to look next?'

'He never said. I went into Belston and we met up and went to the garage'.

She stopped. Sheila said, 'I know this is the bad part for you, Sylvie, but it really will help us if you can tell us what happened at the garage'.

For a moment I thought that more tears were coming, but Sylvia gulped them back and began again.

'When we first got there, we tried the door,

and I was calling Sean, but there was no answer and the door was locked. I said he couldn't be in there . . .' She gulped again and went on. 'Charlie said we ought to check inside and I asked him how and he said he thought he could get on the roof. I helped him and he got up the side. I couldn't see what he was doing, I could just hear him crawling about up there. Then I heard him sliding one of the roof slabs and calling out to Sean. After that he climbed down. He looked really upset and said that Sean was inside and something must have happened to him'.

She gulped again and gave her eyes a quick wipe with Sheila's tissue. 'I said 'What do you mean—something's happened to him?" He said, "He's lying in the car. I think he's had an accident". Then he said, "I think he might be dead". I just went off at that. I was screaming and crying and I remembered beating at poor Charlie and then I don't really remember anything until the police came. They took me home'.

She stopped abruptly, and Sheila shot me a warning glance, to indicate that we'd gone far enough in that direction.

There was a pause, then Sheila said, 'Did anyone ever take a statement from you, or ask you to attend the Inquest?'

Sylvia shook her head. 'No', she said. 'I wanted to go to the Inquest, but my mother thought I shouldn't. I wish I had now. They seem to have said all sorts of things about Sean that weren't true'.

'What about Charlie?' Sheila asked. 'What sort of bloke was he?'

'Charlie? He was a fool. He and Sean had been mates since primary school, always gone around together. They'd played music together. Charlie was weird, though'.

'In what way weird?' I asked.

'He used to imagine things all the time. Nothing was ever the way it is to Charlie. He always imagined something else. If we went to a film, when we came out he'd be imagining things that weren't in the film'.

'What did the song "She Moved Through The Fair" mean to him?' Sheila said.

Sylvia looked blank. 'He loved it', she said, 'but what's it got to do with anything?'

'Take my word for it, there's a reason', said Sheila.

'He just loved that song. He was always singing and whistling it, but like I said, he wasn't happy with the story. You know the story in the song?' she asked.

Sheila nodded. 'A boy courts a girl who's socially above him, but she agrees to marry him. Then she dies, but her ghost comes back and tells him that he's going to die soon and they'll be together'.

'Right', agreed Sylvia, 'That's what everyone makes of the song, but Sean didn't. He used to say that, after the boy and girl met at the fair, the girl was killed by a jealous rich admirer, and her ghost came to warn the boy that the killer was going to get him too, but it didn't matter because then they'd be together'.

'Did you believe his version?' I asked.

'No, of course not. It's obvious in the song. The girl's ill and doesn't tell the boy. Then she dies. That's the "secret that never is shared", that she's ill'.

Sheila nodded, thoughtfully. 'You know', she said, carefully, 'that Charlie's dead, don't you?'

'Yes', Sylvia said, quietly. 'Poor Charlie. He was lost without Sean. Charlie was such a fool. Sean was always like a big brother to him'.

Suddenly I realised what Sheila was going to do, and I made frantic eye signals to try and prevent her. She ignored me and pressed on.

'It hasn't been in the papers yet', she said, 'but Charlie didn't kill himself'.

Sylvia's head came up with a jerk and her big black eyes were wide and startled.

'You mean he was killed—murdered?' she gasped.

'Yes', said Sheila. 'He was'.

There was a long pause while the girl stared and tried to digest this. Then she said, 'So—do you mean that Sean was murdered?'

'Yes', said Sheila.

CHAPTER TWENTY-TWO

We had the row in the car on the way home. I don't like rowing with Sheila, partly because I usually lose and partly because my ex-wife could take a difference of opinion about a TV programme and parlay it into an epic row, which would run for weeks.

I suppose I started it.

'You shouldn't have told her that Sean was murdered', I complained, when we were only just out of Tom's drive.

'Why not?'

'Because he wasn't'.

'Was too', she said.

'What do you mean? I thought we agreed that he died by accident?' I protested.

'No, cobber. You and John Parry and the Doc agreed that he died by accident, but not one of you can explain how that accident happened'.

'Oh, come on', I said. 'He and Sylvia were making love in the car. We know that, right?'

'Right', she agreed.

'It was a chilly evening. Perhaps they had the engine running, to keep warm'.

'They were teenagers', snorted Sheila. 'They didn't need to run the motor to keep warm. They'll do it in three feet of snow when the urge moves them. Anyway, she never said the engine was running'.

'We never asked her', I pointed out.

'You never asked her, Sherlock—so we don't know'.

'OK, so maybe they didn't. But, anyway, she leaves to catch her bus and shuts the garage door behind her...'

'Yair', Sheila interrupted, 'and an experienced mechanic—an experienced mechanic who's worked in that garage with the door shut—sits in his car and turns on the engine to keep himself warm and accidentally kills himself!'

'Right!' I said. 'That's exactly it. He's relaxed after sex. The cold air gets to him and he switches on the engine. Then he just sits there and passes out. It's odourless, you know, carbon monoxide. That's why so many people get lumbered by it'.

'You', she said, 'are lumbered with a theory that won't stand up, and you know it. Sean McBride was murdered. Sylvia knows it'.

'She thinks she knows it', I complained. 'But that's because you told her so'.

'I told her so because it's bloody true, but she already knew it. She just didn't know that she knew it'.

'That's about as clear as the philosophical mixture of guesswork and mathematics you were trying on John Parry the other night', I said.

'If', she said, 'you had been listening to what

Sylvia Wellington said, and remembering what we know about Sean's death, you might have caught on'.

I didn't understand that, so I changed my attack.

'Don't you think that you should have kept your opinions from the girl?' I asked. 'She's screwed up enough about Sean's death, anyway'.

'Don't come the raw prawn with me, cobber! It was you who thought she'd be better off knowing that he didn't top himself. Now she knows that she wasn't responsible in any way, that it wasn't even a stupid accident. Now she knows that some bastard killed her bloke and she can get angry. That's got to be better for her'.

'If it's true', I said.

'Of course it's bloody true!' she snapped. 'Now, stop talking rubbish and direct me out of these backblocks'.

I shut up and settled for the small satisfaction of knowing that she'd taken a wrong turning.

CHAPTER TWENTY-THREE

There was no argument about who prepared supper when we got home—I did. While I was doing so, Sheila delved into my briefcase for the McBride file and sat at the dining table with the file in front of her and a bottle of Talisker alongside. I got the feeling that she was shotting her guns ready to blow me out of the water.

The meal passed in almost total silence. Sheila closed the file before eating, but it still lay close to her, presumably as a warning to me that I hadn't got away with it.

The meal finished, Sheila poured me a large glass of malt, lifted her own and smiled at me. I could have been fooled by the smile, but I could see that her freckles were still standing out darkly, which only happens when she's angry or frightened and she certainly didn't look frightened.

'Now then', she began, 'let me just review the essential facts in the case of Sean McBride and Charlie Nesbit'.

'Are they the same case?' I asked, as innocently as I could.

She showed her teeth. 'Let us, for the moment, assume that they are connected'.

'Very well', I agreed.

'Right, then. Sean McBride is a great, long-time mate of Charlie Nesbit. Sean is courting Sylvia Wellington. Charlie occasionally acts as a go-between. Sean and Sylvie often meet and pursue their purposes at Sean's garage. On the weekend in question, they are planning a dirty weekend away in a hotel. Shortly before that weekend, Sean's home is broken into, but nothing, apparently, is stolen. Right?'

'Right', I agreed, 'but what has that got to do with it?'

'What has what got to do with what?'

'What has the break-in at Sean's home got to do with the deaths of either Sean or Charlie?'

'If you'll shut up, we shall see'.

'Does that mean you don't know?'

'Not at this moment', she admitted, glowering, 'but we shall see. Now—Sylvie decides to see Sean on the Friday evening, and phones Charlie. Charlie tells Sean . . .'

'He told the Coroner that he didn't', I interrupted.

'He was lying', she said. 'Charlie told Sean, and Sean went to the garage. He was probably going there anyway, because he had to replace the passenger seat of the car, ready for the trip the next day. Sylvie meets him at the garage and a good time is had by all until about ten thirty, when Sylvie leaves, dropping the garage door behind her so that it locks. Right?'

'Right', I agreed.

She looked at me, obviously expecting an argument. After a moment she continued. 'Sean, in a state of post-coital euphoria, sprawls in the rear seat of the car and lights a cigarette . . .'

'Is the engine running at this point?' I interjected.

'We don't know', she said. 'It may have been

running while they were fooling about, or he might have switched it on afterwards'.

'Seems to me that this summary contains a lot of "We don't knows"', I remarked.

'Kindly', she said, 'shut your face until I have finished, when you may put any intelligent question that occurs to you or make valid comments. Now—at some point after Sylvie leaves the engine is definitely running. I don't think it matters when it started. The fact is that the garage filled with invisible, odourless, poisonous gas and young Sean quietly died without even knowing it. Right?'

'Right'.

'On the morning after Sean's death, his good friend Charlie trots into his Building Society office and deposits a wad of rhino'.

'Rhino?' I queried.

'Boodle, oof, spondulix, bread, money', she explained. 'What was that for and where did it come from?'

'Maybe someone paid Charlie for getting them what they couldn't find when they broke into Sean's place', I suggested. 'After all, he was certain on that Friday evening that Sean was out'.

'Yair', she said, 'and if you believe Kath, he also knew that Kath was at home doing Sean's laundry, so he'd hardly have gone and broken in'.

'Perhaps he tipped off someone else', I suggested.

'Perhaps not', she said. 'So far as we know, Kath's place was only burgled once and nothing was taken'.

'What do you think they were looking for?' I asked.

'I don't know', she said, then shot a fierce glance across the table. 'Don't say it!' she commanded.

I swallowed my comment. Sheila took another drink and went on. 'So far, we have a dead youngster in that garage—a boy who knew about cars and who had often worked in that garage with the door closed, but who somehow managed to get gassed by exhaust fumes. Then, on Tuesday morning, Charlie wants to go and have a look at the garage.

'Why?'

'He told Sylvia that they should start from where Sean was last seen', I reminded her.

'I know that, and it doesn't make sense. He knew that Kath had already been there and not found Sean, so why go again?'

'Because he knew how to get in if the place was locked?' I hazarded.

She pointed a finger. 'Right!' she said, with a surprised intonation. 'Exactly right, cobber. Doesn't that suggest he knew—or at least thought it possible—that something had happened to Sean in the garage?'

'I don't know', I admitted.

She smiled, dazzlingly. 'Well, bloody well', she said, and went on. 'When they found the door still locked, Charlie climbed on the roof, right?'

'Right', I agreed again.

'Then he shifted one of the roof slabs and looked into the garage and saw Sean's leg sticking out of the car. Yes?'

'Yes', I said, bewildered.

'That's why I said that Sylvie knew that her bloke was murdered', Sheila said. 'She just didn't know that she knew'.

Now I was completely at a loss. 'I give up', I said.

'You give up too bloody easily. Look!' she commanded, and pushed the file across the table. 'Look at the police photos of the garage'.

I pulled them out and went through them. Sheila waited, with growing impatience.

'You can't see it, can you?' she demanded at last.

I shook my head.

'And you don't remember Sylvie saying it, either'.

'Saying what?' I appealed, now totally bemused.

She spoke very slowly, as though addressing an idiot. 'Sylvie said that, when Charlie took her to the garage, he said he believed he could get in. He climbed on the roof and she heard him moving one of the roof slabs. Right?'

'Yes. That's how he looked in and saw Sean and that's how the police got in'.

'Look!' she said, and stabbed a finger at one of the photos. It was a general view of the garage from above, evidently taken from a window in the adjacent tower block. On the roof of the little garage one of the asbestos slabs lay loose, alongside a gap in the roof.

'There's the slab that Charlie moved, and there's the space he made to look through'.

'Yes', I said, 'but . . .'

'But nothing, cobber. Now look at that rectangular mark on the roof, by the hole. That's the mark where the loose slab used to lie. That's where rainwater made a dirt deposit around the edges of the slab while it lay there so that there was always a ventilation gap in the garage roof'.

She grinned triumphantly, as my mind slowly came up to speed.

'You mean . . .' I began.

'I mean, mate, as I have been telling you for hours, that Sean kept that slab loose and pulled aside as a ventilator. The night he died, some bastard climbed on the roof and pushed it back into place so that he died. That's why Charlie had to move it when he got on the roof'.

'Wouldn't he have heard if someone climbed on the roof?'

'Not if they did it while Sean and Sylvie were rocking and rolling. Take it from me, Chris Tyroll, Sean McBride was murdered, and Charlie was either a part of it or he came to know it afterwards'.

CHAPTER TWENTY-FOUR

Mulvaney passed an envelope across my desk. 'There it is', he said, 'the next instalment'.

I counted the notes in the envelope, took out a printed pad and wrote him a receipt. Normally I enjoy receiving bundles of cash from clients, but the fact that Mulvaney's action was being supported by contributions collected by his former workmates was beginning to depress me.

He saw the expression on my face as I passed him the receipt. 'What's the trouble?' he asked. 'It's what we agreed, isn't it?'

'Oh, sure. That's not the trouble. I just don't like the idea of all those working blokes having to chip in to support this action'.

'If there's no other way, they'll do it', he said firmly. 'They've kept it up so far, haven't they?'

'They have', I agreed, 'but I can see this taking a long time in the Tribunal. This isn't just one bloke who's been sacked for one reason. This is three of you who were sacked for a mixture of three reasons. There are five separate cases to be presented here really, with the evidence and arguments to back each one. I hate to think how long it will take, and you won't be paying me for a couple of interviews a week and a bit of back-up work, you'll be paying for day after full day in the hearing, plus conferences and interviews on top. It'll end up costing a bomb, Con'.

'You told us that from the start', he said. 'If the strike had gone on we'd have had to stick it out and put up with short commons. We can stick this out, too'.

'You might have won the strike in the end', I said.

'We might have bloody lost it, too', he said. 'Strikes are like horse races—favourites go lame and outsiders romp home. I suppose Tribunal cases are like that, aren't they?'

'Any case is, before any tribunal', I agreed. 'We'd better hope the outsider wins this time'.

He grinned over his pipe. 'So the odds are that bad, are they?'

'They are for you', I said. 'So far as I can see you called an illegal strike, quite apart from bashing the boss'.

He grinned again. 'Well, you prove the strike was legal and I'll prove I thumped Bailey in self-defence'.

'Right', I said and reached for a notepad. 'We'd got as far as the beginning of the strike. Carry on from there'.

He drew on his pipe. 'I told you about all the strikes there'd been before, well, BDS kept claiming that those strikes had been organised in such a way as to cause the maximum damage'.

'How do you mean?'

'They said that workers had just downed tools and walked out, often in the middle of a continuous process, so that there were incomplete processes and materials lost. They were beginning to hint that there were political reasons for the strikes and since they were a Government defence plant, then political strikes that lost production and wasted materials were akin to sabotage and so on'.

'But that wasn't the case with your strike, was it?'

'You're bloody right it wasn't', he said. 'Personally I think that an employer whose management is so bad that it provokes the workers to walk out ought to put up with any damage caused by their own bad practice, but I wasn't going to have that old story used against us in the press'.

'So, what did you do?'

'I made it absolutely clear, when we fixed the beginning of the strike, that no section would come out until all production in its hands was complete, so that there couldn't be any accusations this time'.

'Did it work?'

'Me and Jimmy were there to make sure it worked. We checked each section personally, to make sure that production was complete and there were no interruptions and no wastage before we told that section to stand down'.

'That must have taken some organising'.

'It did. All day, Jimmy and I kept going back in and taking another section and making sure it could shut down clean, without wastage. That's what caused the fight'.

'How so?' He drew on his pipe. 'Well', he said, 'we'd notified the strike in proper form and we told everybody to turn up for their shift on the day'.

'Did they?'

'Most of them. There's always a few idle buggers who think that a strike is a holiday, but virtually all the usual people clocked on for their shift. So Jimmy Martin and I got started. We went through each section and had a talk with its Shop Steward. We sorted out with them how long it would take their schedule to finish the work they had immediately in hand, without touching any new, incoming stuff. Then we worked out a list of when we expected that section to shut down. We told our people in each section as they weren't to down tools until the present work was all complete and they weren't to leave anything in a state that would cause wastage'.

'Was that always possible? Weren't there any continuous processes?'

He nodded. 'Some', he agreed. ' We told them to shut down properly, like they were closing for an annual holiday, leave nothing out of place, you know?'

I nodded. 'So you had a schedule of when each section was going to shut down, right?'

'Right. Then Jimmy and I and a couple of the other Stewards went across the road to the cafe opposite the gate. We had a late breakfast and a bit of a chat about how we thought the strike'd go and the others went off, so there was just Jimmy and me'.

'How long were you there?'

'We was there all day', he said. 'We had the list of when each section should finish and we'd told the Stewards to come across and let us know as their section was cleared. We'd see the people from that section coming out the gate and the Steward would come across and confirm that they were finished and that it was all done properly'.

'So how did you get into a punch-up at the gate? Your letter of dismissal says you attacked Bailey inside the gate, after being required to leave the premises'.

'I was getting to that', he said. 'Some of the sections were slower than we expected. If we hadn't seen them coming out when we expected them, we'd give it a few minutes, then we'd go over and see what was keeping them'.

'Why was that?'

'Because we wanted the strike solid', he said. 'Some sections were more solid than others, and we wanted to be sure that no section could carry on working'.

'I thought you said that the general meeting was unanimous for a strike?'

'It was, but the sort who'll back down on a strike don't go to general meetings, so we needed to be sure, not just that all production had stopped properly but that it couldn't be restarted'.

I paused in my note-taking and looked up.

'When you give evidence', I said, 'you'd better just say that you were extremely anxious to ensure that your instructions about not wasting production were obeyed. If you say you were checking on absolute solidarity and making sure that production couldn't go on, some of the Tribunal might think that sounds like you were piling on the last straw if you could'.

'Well, I was', he said.

'I'm sure you were. Just don't say it in evidence, that's all'.

He snorted. 'I thought you wanted the truth'.

'I do. I want all the truth, but your pals are paying me to present your case as well as I can to the Tribunal. That means that I decide which bits of the truth make the story look best'.

'Sounds bloody tricksy to me', he grunted. 'I don't mind telling them the truth and taking me chance'.

I put down my ballpen. 'Look', I said, 'any

worker's chance before a Tribunal is a bad one. In presenting your case I've got to make them believe that you acted as any reasonable person would have done, that there was no emotion, no malice, no secret agenda, that you weren't under orders from anywhere else, that you just did what you had to do, right? So take the advice your mates are paying for. Now get on telling me about the fight'.

'It wasn't a fight', he said, 'not as such'.

'He says you thumped him. You say you did, but it was in self-defence. It may have been only a little fight, but it was a fight'.

'Alright', he said. 'Like I explained, Jimmy and me were keeping an eye on the shutdown of each section, and a couple of times we went into the works to see what was keeping them'.

'What sort of security is there on the gate?'

'Security? There's George Barlow on the gate. He's an ex-copper, been with BDS for years'.

'And he didn't stop you going in?'

He shook his head. 'Not the first couple of times. The first time we went in he asked us what we wanted, but he was alright when we told him. He just told us not to be too long about it'.

'He didn't think you were coming in to do any mischief—to guarantee that there *was* wastage, for example?'

'No, of course not. We told him what we were about and he believed us. Then, the third time we went to the gate, about noon, George said we couldn't come in. He said he'd had orders from the front office to keep us out'.

'Why was that?'

'He said as Bailey—the Managing Director—had said we were coming in to threaten people who were unwilling to join the strike and he wasn't having any more of it'.

'What did you do?'

'Well, I told George that he knew quite well why we were coming in and he said he did, but he'd got his orders so we couldn't come in. He was quite alright about it, he's a reasonable bloke is George, but he'd been told and he wasn't going to go against his orders'.

'So, did you leave?'

'Well, we were still talking to George when we heard someone shouting. We looked around and saw Bailey at the window of his office. That's on the ground floor of the front building, about fifty yards from the gate. He had the window open and he was shouting and waving at us'.

'What was he shouting?'

He shook his head. 'I don't really know, we couldn't hear properly. He sounded like he was raving and I suspect it was just a lot of abuse. We just ignored him and he slammed the window to. The next thing we knew he was shouting at us again, but nearer this time. He'd come out of the office and he was running across the tarmac towards the gate. He was waving his arms and yelling at us again'.

'Was there anyone with him?'

'Yes. There were a couple of blokes running after him. One was a bloke called Cheetham—he's a foreman in one of the machine shops, a real dyed-in-the-wool anti-Union company man—and the other was Cantrell'.

'Who's he?'

'The new security manager. When we took the Retaliator on there was a lot of scuttle about security and BDS brought in a contract firm to handle it. Cantrell's their manager. He's always sneaking around with Bailey. The lads call him "Bailey's bloodhound"'

'What happened when Bailey ran across?'

'Well, Jimmy and I was still by the gate, talking to George. He said, "You'd best go, lads. Bailey's got his arse on fire and there's his bloodhound with him", so we told him good day and we turned to go. Just then Bailey arrives at the gate and grabs me by the shoulder and swung me round'.

'He grabbed hold of you?'

'Yes. He took hold of my shoulder and pulled me round to face him'.

'Where were you at that point? Were you inside or outside the gate?'

'I don't honestly recall. I suppose we was outside. We'd stood in the gateway talking to George Barlow and then moved off. I'd have thought we was outside when Bailey grabbed me, does it matter?'

'It may matter as to whether you were trespassing when he laid his hand on you. Did he say anything when he grabbed you?'

'Yes. He said something like, "Barlow, I've told you to keep this scum out of my works! I'm not having them sabotaging product and spreading their bloody strike!"'

'What sort of mood was he in?'

Mulvaney laughed. 'Mood?' he said. 'He was pissed!'

'Pissed?'

'That's right. You could smell it on his breath. He was reeking of it. Once he'd bawled poor old George out, he started on me, telling me I was scum and a traitor. I remember he said that a sensible country would have locked me up for what I was doing'.

'Did you make any reply?'

He laughed again. 'I'm not much for getting into shouting matches with drunks, Chris, but when he'd finished I simply said that George knew why Jimmy and I had been coming back to the works and that was exactly to avoid any unneccessary loss of product'.

'What then?'

'Then he snarled at me that I was a "smug, hypocritical bastard" and hit me in the face'.

'And you hit him back?'

He nodded. 'I certainly did. I ain't going to stand around and let any drunk take a poke at me, Chris, Works Manager or not'.

'Had he injured you when he hit you? Had

he bruised you? Broken the skin?'

He shook his head. 'He didn't break the skin, but I had a damn good bruise for a few days after'.

'Did you injure him?'

'I hope so. I punched him in the mouth and I think a couple of his teeth went. He was bleeding at the mouth afterwards'.

'And what was everyone else doing while you and Bailey were slugging it out? Did Jimmy get involved? Or Mohammed?'

'Mohammed wasn't even there. He was never with us that day. After he hit me no one did anything. George Barlow said something like, "You shouldn't do that, Mr Bailey" and Jimmy shouted something, but Cantrell and Cheetham just stood there. Then, after I'd poked him back, George jumped in between us and Cantrell and Cheetham got hold of Bailey and held him back. George said to me, "Go on, Con. This is no good. Go away from here before it gets worse"'.

'And you left?'

'That's right. We went back across to the cafe. George came over after a bit and said that Bailey was raving mad about me and was swearing he'd have me, and Cantrell was saying not to worry, he'd fix the pair of us'.

'So, what it amounts to is that you and Jimmy Martin approached the gate and asked George to let you pass, as he had done previously. He told you that he'd been instructed not to let you in again, yes?'

'Right'.

'If George had refused you admission the first time, would you have tried to go in?'

'Of course not. I'd have asked him to write down in the Gate Book that we'd asked to come in to ensure that there was no sabotage of product and that we'd been refused. That's what I was saying to him when Bailey arrived'.

'So there should be a record of the scrap between you and Bailey in the Gate Book, yes?'

'There is'. He bent down and took a couple of photocopies out of his briefcase, passing them across the desk to me. They were copies of two pages of a lined ledger, with times entered in the left margin. They read:

1130 hrs: Chairman of Shop Stewards Mulvaney and Steward Martin requested admission. Reason was to check that D Section was completing all plastics treatment before standing down.

ADMITTED for 15 mins. GB.

1142 hrs: Mulvaney & Martin OUT.

1143 hrs: D Section shift OUT.

1215 hrs: Phone from Mr Cantrell. Mr Bailey says that no Shop Stewards are to be admitted again for any reason. GB.

1240 hrs: Mulvaney & Martin request admission to check stand down of E Section. Told them I could not admit them in the light of Mr Bailey's order. Mr Bailey appeared at his office window and shouted something unintelligible. Mulvaney asked me to record my refusal in Book which I agreed. Mr Bailey arrived as Mulvaney and Martin were leaving, seized Mulvaney by shoulder and shouted abusive words at him. I tried to calm situation down. Mulvaney explained why he wanted admission. Mr Bailey uttered more abuse and struck Mulvaney in the face. Mulvaney hit him back. I intervened and Mr Cantrell and Foreman Cheetham restrained Mr Bailey. I advised Mulvaney and Martin to leave, then phoned for Nurse to attend Mr Bailey, who was bleeding at the mouth. Mr Cantrell repeated instruction that no Union officers were to be admitted till further notice. GB.

1251 hrs. E Section Shift OUT.

I looked up from reading it. 'Looks good', I said, 'but it doesn't record your observation that Bailey was drunk and it doesn't mention that Mohammed wasn't there'.

'Have a heart, Chris! It's a bloody wonder George wrote down what he did. If he'd said that Bailey was drunk Cantrell would have had him taken out and shot. As to Mohammed, I suppose George didn't mention him because he wasn't there'.

'I suppose that makes sense'.

CHAPTER TWENTY-FIVE

Sheila and I invited John Parry to eat with us, so that we could break the bad news to him—that Sean McBride had been murdered and that there most probably was a connection with Charlie Nesbit's death. He was not a happy man.

He glowered at us over his glass. 'I should have known', he said, 'that when lawyers come bearing free meals there's a twist in it somewhere. Have you run out of clients? Have you nothing better to do than potter about cluttering up my patch with murder cases? Couldn't you take up stamp collecting or something?'

'Don't blame me', I said. 'It was Sheila who put the pieces together'.

He shook his head, sadly. 'You used to be such a nice lass when you first came to England. What ever happened to bring about this morbid instinct for finding murders?'

'I fell into bad company', said Sheila brightly, pointing at me.

'I thought', he said, 'that your time was gainfully employed in trying to screw the management of BDS on behalf of a bunch of lefty traitors. How's it going?'

'Well, it's going. We start the hearing next Monday'.

'And have you got it all wrapped up?'

I shook my head. 'It's never all wrapped up when you go to a hearing, John. You know that. It's like horse racing—favourites fall and outsiders come up at the last minute. You can do all the preparation you like, you think you've mastered all the facts, read all the law . . .'

'Rehearsed all your witnesses', he said, *sotto voce*.

'. . . worked out brilliant cross-examinations', I continued, ignoring his sarcasm, 'and then someone says the wrong thing, or forgets to say the right thing, and the whole damn thing falls apart. And it's worse in a Tribunal'.

'Why's that?' Sheila asked.

'Because they allow people to give hearsay evidence'.

'What's that?'

'In the criminal courts, witnesses are only allowed to testify about what they actually know—what they have personally seen, heard, experienced. They can't say that they know something because someone else told them. That would be hearsay evidence. In the Tribunals, that kind of rubbish is accepted as evidence'.

'So you're not looking forward to Monday?' John asked.

'Not hardly, no. I shall walk in there on Monday morning and find that I'm up against some hugely famous QC that BDS are paying three grand a day to mau-mau my clients and their witnesses, and the Tribunal will smarm all over him because he's so bloody famous, and he'll have fifteen assistants with him armed with laptops and stacks of law books, and I shall be there with . . .'

'. . . just me and my trusty notebook and pencil', piped up Sheila.

'Look on the bright side, boyo', said Parry. 'You're always telling me about the old fossils who serve on the Tribunals and how some of them sleep half the time. Just get Sheila to pick the sleepiest and smile at him every time he opens his eyes—that'll get you one vote out of three'.

'Pommy chauvinist!' she said, and punched him in the arm.

'It wouldn't work, anyway', I said. 'The old sleepers on the Tribunals only do it so they can get paid for staying away from their wives. The last thing they want to think about is women'.

John drained his glass. 'Duw, Duw', he said. 'I am going home now, before the prevailing gloom infects my otherwise happy and equable nature. Best of luck on Monday, boyo, or break a leg or whatever lawyers wish each other before a case'.

What lawyers wish each other before a case is usually a spectacular failure so the business will come to them next time, but no matter. I suppose it was well meant.

The Employment Tribunal sits in a faceless

office block in the centre of Birmingham, holding its hearings in bland, featureless rooms, furnished with anonymous tables and cheap office chairs. Con, Jimmy and Mohammed had already found their way to the right room before Sheila and I arrived and were waiting for us in the corridor.

'The BDS crew are already in there', Con said, 'but I haven't seen their lawyer'.

'He'll probably come sweeping in at the next to last moment', I said, 'all black jacket and striped pants, with a retinue of clerks and pupils carrying his books, just to make an impact from the start'.

I was wrong. Inside the hearing room a knot of what I took to be BDS people occupied the far end of the lawyers' tables at the front and, as I walked in, one of them detached himself from the group and approached me with an outstretched hand.

'Mr Tyroll?' he said, smiling affably, 'My name is Maddox. I'm the Deputy Head of Legal Services at BDS. I'm presenting the firm's case'.

Deputy Head? I thought. Not even the Head. No flashy QCs. No—they were so bloody confident that they hadn't bothered. They didn't think that this case was worth spending the money on, it was so obviously a winner for them.

I smiled back at him and gripped his hand with what I hoped was a firm and confident clasp. 'Good morning', I said, 'I thought you might have brought in a hired gun'.

He shook his head. 'No, no. Management thinks I ought to do it, so here I am. You'll have to excuse me if my Tribunal procedure is a bit rusty'.

'As long as your evidence is too', I said, 'we shan't mind a bit'.

'Who's he?' Sheila whispered as we spread our books and papers at the near end of the lawyers' tables.

'He's a company solicitor from BDS. He's presenting their case'.

'Ha!' she said, 'No big QC's. They're afraid of wasting their money'.

'Don't you believe it. They think they can win even if the under assistant teaboy runs the case'.

'Stop talking yourself into a funk, Chris Tyroll. You've got an audience at the back and it looks like the blokes who are paying for all this'.

I turned and looked at the three rows of uncomfortable chairs provided for the public. Most of the seats were full and Con, Jimmy and Mohammed were standing by them, chatting to the occupants. The blokes at BDS had paid their piper and now at least some of them had come to hear the tune.

The press table at the back of the room was full, which surprised me. Normally the media ignores the administrative tribunals, and the most I recalled seeing was one local freelance, who usually reported the boss' side of the evidence and ignored the rest. Today he shared the table with two colleagues, both of them strangers to me. Obviously the tabloids were going to get their mileage out of my clients.

A thin-faced, drably dressed female clerk brought a bundle of papers to her desk in front of the Tribunal's raised bench, sorted them and left through a back door. Moments later she was back, leading in the members of the Tribunal.

The chairman I had seen before. A small, plump, fussy little man, who advertised his legal status, even in this supposedly informal hearing, by wearing the barrister's uniform of black jacket and striped trousers. On his left was a large, broadfaced man, with swept back silver hair, a light tan and an expensive suit. Him I took to be the representative of a management association. The last member to sit was a thin, red-faced man with tufty white hair and watery eyes, apparently the trade union member of the trio.

'Then the Crowner he come and the justice too, with a hue and a cry and a hullabaloo', Sheila muttered, in a bad imitation Berkshire accent.

The clerk looked at Sheila and me severely, then made a short announcement about the procedure to be followed, and the show was under way.

Maddox called his first witness, Bailey the Managing Director. I was pleased to note that he was larger than Con Mulvaney. I had feared that he might be some little old man that only a maniac would punch, but he was over six feet tall and broad-shouldered, though running to fat. Under thick black hair, his wide pale face showed a thin, hard mouth and two equally hard black eyes.

Maddox lead his witness through his name and status, together with an outline of his history with BDS, which Bailey had joined as a teenager. Then he went off on what I thought to be a strange tack.

'You've told us about yourself', he said, 'and your relationship with BDS. Could you tell us a little about the company itself? It's very old, I believe?'

'Fairly old, yes', said Bailey. 'It was formed in the 1840s as a simple partnership called Bailey and Wadsworth. The Bailey in question was a direct ancestor of mine'.

That drew an approving nod from the chairman, as though being descended from a Victorian entrepreneur automatically made Bailey a better witness.

'What did that partnership produce, Mr Bailey?'

'It was simply a small supplier of specialist ammunition, for sporting purposes, shotgun shells and so on, but it diversified and began to produce military ammunition'.

'I believe it changed its name about then'.

'Yes, indeed. It became the Staffordshire Ammunition Company, and continued to trade under that name into this century'.

'And it increased in size, quite considerably I think?'

'That's right. With Government contracts it opened several factories and diversified into the production of larger shells, so that by the time of the South African war it was a major supplier of artillery shells'.

'That's the Boer War? About a century ago?'

Before Bailey could answer I rose. Maddox paused and looked at me with surprise. The chairman frowned. 'Mr Tyroll?' he said.

'Sir, I intervene merely to enquire if there is a purpose in this history of BDS. If Mr Maddox proposes to take us through every development in the armaments industry over the past century we shall be here for a very long time'.

The chairman looked enquiringly at Maddox. 'I can assure Mr Tyroll that I have no such intention, Mr Chairman. I was merely trying to give the Tribunal a little background on the nature of the company'.

The chairman looked at me again. 'Sir', I said, 'we are not concerned with the history or nature of BDS. We are concerned with its present industrial relations and with the particular events surrounding last spring's strike and the dismissals of my clients. When I call my clients, I shall not be asking them for their entire life histories, nor for the history of their Union, merely for their recollection of the events around which this hearing revolves'.

The chairman pursed his small mouth. 'Nevertheless, Mr Tyroll', he said, 'I feel it may help us to have a little background to the specific events which we must consider and I propose to allow Mr Maddox to continue'.

His colleague on the left nodded. The third member was already looking dozy. I didn't blame him. Still, I'd tested the water and confirmed that Maddox was going to be given latitude. I doubted that I would meet the same consideration. Maddox continued:

'As the Staffordshire Ammunition Company, the firm expanded even further during the Great War, isn't that the case?'

'Very much so. We supplied not only the British forces but also Empire and Allied armies and navies'.

I recalled briefly the British-made shells supplied to Russia in that war, which had cases of foil-covered cardboard instead of brass, because much of the purchasing funds had gone into back pockets, and I wondered if one of the illustrious Baileys had taken his ill-gotten share.

The mention of the Empire had won another approving nod from the chairman, and a wave to Maddox to carry on.

'The period between the two World Wars was, as we all know, a difficult time economically, but perhaps you can tell us a little about how your company fared, Mr Bailey?'

'Certainly. Consolidation was necessary, and a number of our wartime factories closed, but the firm became a public company as Stamco Limited, under which name we continued to trade until the 1950s'.

'And during the Second World War the company was, again, a major supplier of weaponry to British and Allied forces?'

Bailey nodded. 'Of course. It was after the War that we were invited by the Government to involve ourselves in the completely new field of missile development—rocketry. The first of what has been a long line of missiles developed by the company was the Firedrake in 1955'.

'And some time after that, the firm changed its name, I think?'

'Yes. In 1965 we amalgamated with British Control Systems and became British Defence Systems—BDS'.

'And BDS is, at present, involved in the production of a major new weapon known as the Retaliator. Now, Mr Bailey I am sure that the Official Secrets Act prevents you from telling us anything about the nature of Retaliator, but can you give the Tribunal some idea of its importance in the defence of this country?'

'Retaliator, as its name implies, will give Britain the opportunity to respond so fast to any attack, that an enemy may well find his positions destroyed before his own weapons have reached us'.

Maddox smiled and nodded. Picking up a news cutting he said, 'So the *Daily Telegraph* was not exaggerating when it said that "Retaliator will safeguard our shores in a way that has never before been possible"?'

'I couldn't have put it better myself', said Bailey with an air of satisfaction, and earned himself another approving nod, not just from the chairman but from his left seated colleague as well.

So, we had BDS established as the defenders of Britain for more than a century and never more so than now. The next move was, I thought, obvious, and I was right.

'Now, Mr Bailey', Maddox went on, 'You heard Mr Tyroll object to my little exploration of the history of BDS, and I am unwilling to give him cause to object again, or'—with a servile smirk to the chairman—'to try the Tribunal's patience much further. Perhaps you would give us a brief summary of the state of labour relations in BDS and its predecessor firms during its long history'.

Bailey drew back in his seat, clasping his hands on the table in front of him and clearing his throat. He was evidently about to make an important (and probably rehearsed) announcement.

'As I understand it', he said. 'The original firm were regarded as generous employers by the standard of Victorian England, and, in the twentieth century, policies to benefit the firm's workers were constantly reviewed and extended. As a result, until recent years, labour relations at BDS were not a problem. The workforce were always well-treated and recognised the national importance of the work we were doing'.

'Do you know, from memory, Mr Bailey, when BDS was first unionised?'

'I can only guess', he replied. 'I believe that it was during or after the First World War'.

'And there has always been union representation in the firm's works' since then?'

'Certainly'.

'Now, the three Applicants in the present matter, although employed in three different sections of the Belston works, are all, in fact, members of the same trade union, the Munitions Industry Union. Can you explain that, Mr Bailey?'

'Of course. By the time of the amalgamation in 1968 we recognised several different unions in our plants. Some people here may recall the period of so-called 'demarcation disputes—' arguments between management and a number of unions in various trades as to which operatives should carry out which task. We did not have that in BDS. It is unnecessarily divisive and highly inefficient. For that reason we moved to recognition of one union only—one that specifically represents workers in the armaments industry'.

'I see', said Maddox, and nodded. 'You said, a moment or two ago, that "until recent years" labour relations had not been a problem at BDS. Can you tell us how things changed?'

Bailey looked thoughtful, then began. 'Commencing a few years ago, we were plagued by a series of instant strikes—wildcat strikes, I believe you would call them'.

'And was the Union involved in this?'

'Oh no, no, not at all. The Union at the time was in complete agreement with BDS that the economic situation required us to keep a tight ship and steer cautiously. The strikes I am talking about were instant action by disaffected workers—immediate walkouts from the shop floor'.

Now, I could have stopped Maddox and his witness here, because none of this had anything to do with Mulvaney or Martin or the strike that Mulvaney called. Maddox was setting it up as prejudicial background before moving on to Mulvaney's strike. As it was, it occurred to me to let it run on, because I believed I could make ammunition (to coin a phrase) out of it later.

'Do you recall how many of these incidents

there were, Mr Bailey?'

'At least twenty, maybe more. They were extremely disruptive. They dislocated our production schedules and caused us problems with customers, they caused loss of product . . .'

'In what way did they cause loss of product?'

'Because they would walk out in an instant, leaving whatever process they were working on unfinished. Chemical treatments that could not be stopped were left incomplete, test runnings that needed to be minutely observed and recorded were left running with no observers, and so on'.

Maddox nodded. 'Virtually a form of industrial sabotage, then?'

I waited three seconds for the chairman to rein him in, knew that it wasn't going to happen and stood up.

'Mr Chairman, we are here to deal with three allegations—that one of my clients disobeyed a legitimate order of Mr Bailey's, that two of them promoted an illegal strike and that all of them assaulted Mr Bailey. Nowhere have I seen it alleged that any of them were engaged in industrial sabotage, least of all in their letters of dismissal'.

The chairman was saved from having to restrain Maddox. The offender was anxious to say that he recognised that his phrase was 'unfortunate' and that he withdrew the question.

Nevertheless, even the chairman thought

that Maddox had had enough latitude.

'You have spent sometime, Mr Maddox, exploring the history of BDS and its labour relations record. Unless there are good reasons for going further in that direction, perhaps you could bring your witness to the events which are the subject of these Applications?'

'Oh, indeed Mr Chairman. I have all the background which I imagine you might need, sir. I shall try to forge ahead'.

He fluttered his hands among the papers on his table, while I wondered if all of BDS were trained in nautical imagery. At last he cleared his throat and began again:

'Mr Bailey, if we might come, as the Tribunal wishes, to the subject of these Applications—I am right, I believe, in saying that the situation arose out of an order given to the Applicant Mohammed Afsar?'

I rose again, before Bailey could answer. 'Mr Chairman', I said, 'While Mr Maddox took us through his excursion into industrial history I made no complaint about the form of his questions, largely because the answers were irrelevant to the cases in hand. If we are, at last, to come to the point, I shall be grateful if my colleague could be asked to abandon his habit of using leading questions'.

Maddox smiled, sardonically. 'I am grateful, I am sure, for Mr Tyroll's forbearance up to this point, and I shall attempt not to try his patience from now on'.

The chairman smiled. 'Thank you, Mr Maddox. At the same time, Mr Tyroll, I would remind you that this is not a Court, it is an administrative Tribunal, and the rules of evidence differ from those with which you may be more familiar. Please proceed, Mr Maddox'.

'What did all that mean?' Sheila whispered.

'He keeps asking leading questions—questions that suggest the answer'.

'No', she hissed, 'I know that bit. What was the rest of it?'

'The rest was a reminder that scruffy little Magistrates' Court advocates like me have no business here.'

Maddox had waited with exaggerated patience for our whisperings to end. Now he launched his questioning again.

'Mr Bailey, all three of the Applicants were dismissed by you on the same day in May of this year. Can you explain to us how that came about?'

Bailey clasped his hands on the table again. 'Yes', he began. 'In May of this year we had a slowing down in the work on Retaliator at our Belston works'.

'A slowing down?'

'Yes. You will appreciate that various processes are carried out at our different premises which come together eventually into a finished product. The Retaliator work was mainly based at Belston, but certain processes were being handled at Coventry. When you have that kind of situation, it is important to try and keep the operations at different plants running in phase, so that there are no unnecessary delays'.

'But that wasn't possible in May?'

'No. Certain work at Coventry took longer than expected, leaving a number of sections at Belston unable to proceed with the next stages of the operation'.

'That must be a matter of great concern to you, something like that happening?'

'It is, of course. Not only does it delay the entire operation, it reduces profitability and, if it goes on long enough, it may cause the laying-off of workers from those sections which cannot proceed. To avoid that, I took a number of measures, one of which was to ask the heads of departments to consider any jobs that needed to be done and which could be tackled while Belston waited for Coventry to come through. One such suggestion came from Mr Greene, who heads the Accounts Section at Belston. He had a long term project which he had mentioned to me on various occasions'.

'And what was that?'

'I don't now recall all the details, but it was to do with computerising certain accounts records which we still held on paper. He had not been able to get it done before because he said that all his operators were fully engaged'.

'And how did you respond?'

'I told him that a large part of the computer section were held up by the delays at Coventry, so that it ought to be possible for him to borrow someone from Mr Swan in Computers who could do the work'.

'And having made that decision, I imagine you didn't expect to hear any more about it?'

'Quite right. I knew that Computers were almost at a standstill, and if all Mr Greene needed was someone who could handle a computer, then it seemed a good time for him to use some of Mr Swan's spare capacity'.

'And what happened next?'

'The next I heard was that Greene had asked Swan for a man and that Swan had asked Mohammed Afsar, who had refused'.

'And what did you do?'

'I telephoned Afsar at once and made clear that it was my decision and that I expected it to be obeyed'.

'And how did he respond?'

'He refused. Told me that he had not been employed as an Accounts Clerk. He refused'.

'And what did you do?'

'I told him that, if he wasn't prepared to do as he was told, I had no use for him at BDS and that he might as well go home'.

'And did he go home?'

'He must have done, because I had a phone call later that day from his father. He tried to suggest that it was all some kind of mistake and suggested that, if his son apologised, I might be prepared to take him back'.

'And how did you respond?'

'I told him that, if his son both apologised and agreed to work in Accounts, I would consider reinstating him'.

'And what happened next?'

'I heard no more of the matter until early in the following week, when Mulvaney and Martin came to see me about Afsar'.

'And what was their point?'

'Mulvaney sought to argue that Afsar had been improperly dismissed. He was very aggressive in putting across his point of view and would not listen to my argument'.

'And what was your argument?'

'That Afsar had been an employee of BDS and thereby obliged to obey any legitimate order of the management. He had quite deliberately refused such an order and I had every right to dismiss him'.

'So, you reached no agreement. Was there any further meeting with any Union representative?'

'Yes. I had another meeting with Mulvaney, but it was the same as the first. He kept saying that Afsar was being made a scapegoat, that I had broken the agreed dismissal and disciplinary procedures and that it was this kind of thing that had led to strikes in the past. I told him that Afsar had quite clearly and deliberately disobeyed an order and that I viewed that as misconduct sufficient to warrant immediate dismissal. We argued this about for some time, but we were getting nowhere. Eventually Mulvaney said that he was going to raise the matter with his Union at a national level'.

'And how did you respond to that?'

'I told him that he must do as he thought best, but I was actually quite pleased. I have always found the Union's national officers—most particularly the Midland Regional Secretary, Mr Goatly—to be reasonable and responsible men with whom one can deal'.

'And you later had a meeting with them?'

'Yes, well, with Mr Goatly. That was a much more successful meeting'.

'In what way?'

'Goatly started off by taking Mulvaney's argument that the dismissal of Afsar was in breach of the disciplinary rules, but he was far less aggressive than Mulvaney had been. I agreed that, in the haste of the moment, I might have overlooked some aspects of the procedure, and we set about finding a solution that was acceptable to both of us'.

'And did you?'

He nodded firmly 'Oh yes. I agreed with Goatly that Afsar could be reinstated as soon as he cared to come back to work'.

'And you no longer demanded an apology, despite Afsar's behaviour to you personally?'

Another leading question, but I let it pass.

'No', said Bailey. 'It seemed to me much more important to end the whole episode satisfactorily rather than to stand on my personal pride'.

A very statesmanlike answer, which earned him a nod from the chairman.

'And, after your meeting with Mr Goatly, you thought that was the end of the matter?'

'Of course. Afsar had his job back if he wanted it. There was nothing further to bother about'.

'But you heard again from the Applicants—from Messrs Mulvaney and Martin?'

'That's right'. Bailey looked pained at the memory. 'They came to see me again and said that they needed to clear up one or two points about Afsar's reinstatement'.

'And which points were those?'

'They wanted an assurance in writing that Afsar's pension and redundancy rights would not be affected by the interruption of his employment. Insofar as it had only been a matter of days, I agreed to that with no argument. Then Mulvaney said, "So, you will be paying him for the days that he's been away?"'

'How did you respond to that?'

'I was very angry. I had bent over backwards to solve what I considered to be a quite minor matter of a disobedient employee, and here they were trying to extract every penny from the situation. I refused, and told that I thought

Afsar was very lucky to have been offered reinstatement, that my terms had been quite acceptable to their Regional Secretary and that I was not prepared to waste any further time on it'.

'How did they respond?'

'Mulvaney said that it wasn't a question of how Goatly viewed it, but how the membership saw it. He said that he was going to call a general meeting of the Union and we would see what the members thought, but it was the sort of thing that had caused strikes in the past. That was the end of our discussion'.

The chairman looked at his watch and muttered something to the clerk, then announced, 'This hearing will now be adjourned until this afternoon'.

The clerk echoed him, 'This hearing is adjourned until 2.15 this afternoon'.

The Tribunal and clerk took their exit from the side door and everyone else began to drift into the corridor, most of us reaching for our cigarettes.

CHAPTER TWENTY-SIX

Outside the hearing room, Maddox was chatting to one of the journalists, so I had no opportunity to ask how long he expected to be with Bailey before I had a chance to cross-examine. Mulvaney and Martin buttonholed me by the lift.

'How much more of this crap have we got to sit through?' Mulvaney demanded.

'You know the game, Con. We put up with however much Maddox wants and the chairman will let him get away with. Then we get our chance'.

'Are you coming for a pint?' asked Martin.

I shook my head. 'No, sorry. The air-conditioning in that room gets at my throat and alcohol will make me sleepy this afternoon. I'm going to go and get some fresh, dusty, petrol-sodden, Brummy air'.

Sheila and I bought sandwiches and soft drinks and headed for the Cathedral churchyard, just around the corner. Although we were well into September, the weather had stayed warm, and we sprawled on the grass of the little churchyard to take our picnic.

Sheila had wandered off to read the inscription on the memorial to the battle of Abu Klea when a voice hailed me.

'Hello, Mr Tyroll. Enjoying the sunshine?'

It was Samson, the man whose ponies I had rescued from the rustler.

'Enjoying a well-deserved break from an Employment Tribunal, actually', I said. 'What brings you to Brum?'

'Oh, it's my day for sorting out all my business in Birmingham. I've got to see someone in Bennett's Hill'.

'You didn't have any more problems over the ponies, did you?'

He shook his head. 'No, no. That was alright. Maiden's Security Manager was a bit awkward about it, and put us to a lot of trouble about picking them up, but we got them in the end and Maiden has let us graze them on his field. We're grateful, Mr Tyroll'.

'No problem, Mr Samson. That's what we're here for—to keep the wolf from the lambs and the rustlers from your ponies'.

He laughed, lifted a hand and ambled away across the green. It was the last time I ever saw him.

Sheila came back and was sitting beside me when another voice greeted me. This time it was one of the three journalists I had seen in the hearing, a tall, hard-faced man with short, greying fair hair.

'Mr Tyroll?' he said. I nodded. 'I'm John Walters', he said. 'I'm a freelance reporter covering your hearing. I wondered', he went on, 'if that was Mr Samson you were talking to?'

I nodded again. 'Do you know him?' I asked.

'Slightly', he said. 'I filed a story about him and his mate's ponies, but it didn't get used'.

'Well, if you want an interview with the legal genius who reactivated a piece of medieval law, now's your chance'.

He grinned and shook his head. 'They

wouldn't run it the first time. It's old news now. So, he was a client of yours, was he?'

'Yes', I said. 'Have you finished in the Tribunal for the day? Have you given all of the bosses' side to the evening papers and you're not going to listen to us?'

He grinned again. 'Oh, I shall be in and out in case you come up with something exciting, Mr Tyroll'.

He waved a hand and strolled away.

'Blimey!' I said. 'If you can't be left alone in a graveyard, where can you?'

We picked up our litter and started back to the hearing.

Maddox reminded Bailey that he was still under oath and away we went.

'Now, Mr Bailey. Before the luncheon adjournment you told us that, at your last meeting with the Applicants, Mulvaney threatened you with a strike'.

I had to rise. 'Mr Bailey said', I objected, 'that Mr Mulvaney had said that this had been the kind of incident that had led to strikes in the past. That is an observation, not a threat'.

'It depends', said the chairman, 'on how Mr Bailey viewed the "observation". Did you take it as a threat, Mr Bailey?'

'I did, sir, particularly coupled with his announcement that he was going to put the matter to his members'.

I subsided. Maddox smiled at me and continued:

'So, Mr Mulvaney threatened a strike and announced that he was calling a general meeting. What occurred next?'

'I was informed that there had been a general meeting of the Union and that there had been a vote taken to ballot the branch for a strike'.

'What did you do?'

'Do? There was nothing I could do except await any action by the Union. Subsequently I received a formal notice that the Union was balloting for a strike'.

Maddox selected a document from his files and passed it across. 'Is this that document?'

'Yes, it is.'

'And did you notice anything unusual about it?'

'I don't know if you would call it unusual. Your office advised me that it was in the proper legal form, but I noticed that it was signed by Mulvaney as Chairman of Shop Stewards for the Belston Branch, not by any national officer of the Union.'

'And wouldn't you say that was unusual?'

'I don't know the Union's rules and procedures, but I would have thought that such a document should have been signed by the National Secretary'.

I rose. 'Mr Chairman, before the witness speculates any further about what he admits he doesn't know, could I ask whether the Respondent has any evidence on this point?'

The chairman looked at Maddox, who smiled happily.

'There will, Mr Chairman, be evidence as to the Union's usual procedures and rules', he said, 'and in the meantime I shall be grateful if the notice of ballot can be entered as a Respondent's Exhibit'.

I sat down and the formalities were gone through before Maddox resumed. On the corner of my notepad I wrote, 'WHO is the Union fink who will give evidence?' I would have to ask Mulvaney for a guess.

'So, Mr Bailey, you had some kind of a notice of the Union ballot. What then?'

'Next I received a notification of the result of the ballot and a notice of the intended strike. That was also signed by Mulvaney'.

'And did you respond?'

'Yes. I did that time. I wrote to Mulvaney, saying that I had received his notice but that I did not regard it as legal and proposed to ignore it'.

Maddox selected two more documents from his file, had Bailey confirm that they were the notice and his reply and had them entered as Exhibits.

'And did you receive any further communication from Mr Mulvaney or from the Union?'

'No, but I phoned Mr Goatly and told him that Mulvaney was, in my view, fomenting an illegal strike'.

'How did he respond?'

'He confirmed my view that the Union had not authorised the ballot or the strike, and said that he would try and stop Mulvaney making any further trouble'.

'Were those his actual words?'

I was up again. 'Mr Chairman, I am aware that hearsay evidence is admissible before this Tribunal, but I suggest that Mr Bailey's account of what Mr Goatly may or may not have said is deeply prejudicial and should not be admitted'.

The chairman considered the complaint for about half a second before replying. 'Mr Tyroll, I have reminded you before that this is an administrative tribunal, not a Court of Law, and that the rules of evidence are different here. No doubt when your own witnesses come to give evidence they will wish to avail themselves of our more realistic rules. Carry on, Mr Maddox'.

Maddox smirked at me. 'Thank you, Mr Chairman'. I made a mental note to stop losing objections. It must look bad to the blokes at the back who were paying for my alleged skills.

'I think we can assist Mr Tyroll by cutting the matter short, Mr Bailey. If he won't object to my leading a little. Mr Goatly I believe, failed to convince Mr Mulvaney and the strike went ahead'.

'That's so, yes'. Bailey looked pained.

'And on the first day of the strike you had a confrontation with the Applicants?'

Bailey looked even more pained. 'Yes. I did. At the gate of the factory'.

'Can you tell us how that came about?'

'Well, on that first day, you will appreciate that we were in a very confused state. At first we did not know how far the strike would be effective and how many men would withdraw their labour. As a result, there was a meeting of senior staff and heads of sections going on in my office, almost continually. We were receiving information every minute of the state of play in different sections of the plant. It came to my notice that Mulvaney and Martin had made a number of visits to the premises and had been admitted by the gate officers. As a result, Mr Cantrell phoned the security officer in charge of the gate and passed on my order that the, er, the Applicants were not to be admitted again for any reason at all'.

'Why was that, Mr Bailey?'

'As I mentioned earlier, during the period of wildcat strikes that we suffered there was what I would call sabotage, irredeemable loss of product and the like'.

I bobbed up quickly. 'That "unfortunate" word again, Mr Chairman'.

Maddox waved a hand in acknowledgement of my complaint. 'So you feared that irredeemable harm would be done by the strikers?'

Bailey nodded firmly. 'Yes, I did. I had hardly issued the order when someone in my office said that they were at the gates now. I should explain that my office is on the ground floor of the front block of the buildings and commands a view of the gate'.

'What did you do?'

'I stood up and it was true. I could see the, er, the Applicants standing at the gate apparently talking to George Barlow, the gatekeeper. I opened the window of my office and I shouted to Barlow to see them off the premises. They looked round, but I didn't see any other reaction, so I asked Mr Cantrell to come with me and we made for the gate. Mr Cheetham, one of the heads of section came with us also'.

'And who is Mr Cantrell?'

'Mr Cantrell is the senior officer of the security contractors who were in the process of taking over our security arrangements at the time'.

'And what happened when you reached the gate?'

'I told Barlow that he was to keep them out. While I was doing so, both Mulvaney and Martin abused me and, as I turned away from Barlow, Mulvaney flung a punch at me and Martin grabbed hold of me. I believe that he punched me as well'.

'Where were you struck?'

'Mulvaney's blow landed in my face, just

below the right eye. I felt another blow, which I believe was from Martin, in my ribs'.

'And then what happened?'

'Mr Cantrell and Mr Cheetham intervened, together with Mr Barlow and drove the, er, Applicants away. The last I saw of them, they were heading towards a cafe across the road from the gate'.

'And were you hurt by their blows? Did you require treatment?'

'Mr Cantrell took me to the Nurse's office, where Nurse Burton examined my injuries and dressed them. I had a black eye for several days after and severe bruising to my ribs'.

'And what did you do then?'

'I returned to my office and dictated letters to all three Applicants, confirming their dismissals. The letters were typed and Mr Cantrell undertook to ensure that they were delivered by hand on the same day'.

Maddox nodded. 'Now, Mr Bailey, we are not really concerned with the events of the strike itself, merely with the events which brought about the dismissal of the Applicants, and you have told us about that. Nevertheless, I think it may assist the Tribunal if you will give us at least a summary of what happened afterwards and how the strike proceeded'.

Bailey went on to tell how, by the end of the first day, most of the Belston plant had closed down. He had made numerous representations to Goatly, who had attempted to persuade the remaining Shop Stewards that they were engaged in an illegal strike, but the strike had remained firm for three weeks. It had been a considerable difficulty for the firm, whose contracts for the Retaliator were with Britain and various other European governments, but who hoped to sell the missile to the United States. The American deal was already under discussion and its success was directly threatened by the strike at Belston.

After three weeks, the strike had spread to BDS's Coventry works, where more than half the workforce had walked out. He had personally drafted a statement to the workers at Coventry, explaining the origins of the Belston strike and that it was illegal. The Union had co-operated in persuading the Coventry strikers back to work and, with the collapse of the Coventry action, the Belston strike ended.

As Bailey finished his recital, the chairman looked at his watch. 'I am certain', he said, with a sarcastic glance at me, 'that Mr Tyroll will wish to cross-examine Mr Bailey at some length, and it does not seem to be wise to embark on that late in the afternoon. This hearing is adjourned to 10.15 tomorrow morning'.

As I had expected, Maddox had filled up the afternoon with rubbish, so that his witness would start cross-examination in the morning, fresh and with the benefit of an evening's preparation behind him.

CHAPTER TWENTY-SEVEN

You can prepare and rehearse a witness to a large extent, but you can't rehearse a cross-examination. It's an art form, not a science. All I could do was pore over Sheila's notes and my own of Bailey's evidence and make sure I had identified all the weak points in his story. Whether I could open them up was another question.

Bailey took his place next morning, the chairman reminded him that he was still under oath, and we were off again.

I decided to go straight for a mystery that had intrigued me the day before.

'Mr Bailey', I began, 'you told us yesterday about the brawl at the gate and that, immediately after you had received medical treatment, you dictated the letters of dismissal. Am I right?'

'Yes'. Someone had obviously told him that there are five answers to cross-examiners—yes, no, I don't know, I don't remember, and I didn't understand the question—and always keep your answers short so as not to give additional information.

'Then the events at the gate must have been very clear in your recollection when the letters were written?'

'Yes. They were'.

I picked up the copies of the letters which had been exhibited on the previous day. 'Now two of these letters are identical. You told both Mr Mulvaney and Mr Martin that, "You have been largely instrumental in fomenting an illegal strike within the Belston plant, you have trespassed on the company's premises and you have assaulted me personally". Do you recall writing that?'

'Yes'.

'Then there is the letter to Mr Afsar. That says, "You deliberately disobeyed a legitimate instruction given by your Head of Section and confirmed by me. In addition, you trespassed upon the company's premises and joined in an assault on me by Mulvaney and Martin". Did you write that?'

'Yes'.

'Why?'

He stared at me, pretending not to understand, and repeated the question while he sought an answer. 'Why? Because those were the facts, that's why'.

'That surprises me, Mr Bailey, because those were not the facts that you recited in evidence yesterday'. He began to speak again, but I pressed on. 'Yesterday you told us that you saw "the Applicants" at the gate, that you went over with your colleagues and that you were struck in the face by Mr Mulvaney and probably in the ribs by Mr Martin. Is that right?'

'Yes'.

'When you kept using the expression "the Applicants" in your account yesterday, to whom were you referring?'

'All three of them—Mulvaney Martin and Afsar'.

'And you saw them all at the gate?'

There was a long pause. Then, 'Mulvaney and Martin were there. They assaulted me'.

'So you say Mr Bailey, so you say, but you also say that Mr Afsar trespassed on the company's premises and assaulted you'.

'That was a mistake', he said, reluctantly.

'A mistake!' I exclaimed loudly 'Two of the three reasons why you were dismissing him were a mistake. Can I ask how you came to make that mistake when the events at the gate were fresh in your memory?'

Maddox sprang up. 'If it will assist Mr Tyroll, I am instructed that an identical text was prepared on a word processor for the letters to Mulvaney and Martin and then varied for Afsar. In that process, and in the confusion of the moment, the text of the letter to Afsar included inappropriate material. I can assure the Tribunal that we do not seek to justify Afsar's dismissal on the grounds of trespass or assault, solely on the question of his refusal of an order'.

I glanced back at the press table, to see that

they were getting all this, and was disappointed to note that Walters and another were missing.

'Thank you', I said. 'I am grateful to Mr Maddox for giving the evidence which his witness was so reluctant to give, and which he strove so hard to conceal yesterday'.

Time to change the topic. Never let a witness answer on one point for too long. It allows them to start guessing at the next question.

'Now', I continued, 'we heard a lot yesterday about the long history of BDS and its predecessors and about its labour relations. I don't wish to go into all of that in detail again, but there are one or two points that I would like to pursue. I think you told us that, throughout its long existence, your company had an excellent record in labour relations until the burst of wildcat strikes a few years ago?'

He relaxed. He'd rehearsed this bit and done it once. 'I think it's fair to say that, yes.'

I picked up a small sheaf of photocopies that Sheila had prepared for me. 'And does your view include the strike by women employees in 1917?'

It was plain from his face that he had never heard of it. 'I don't know what you mean', he said.

'I mean that, in 1917, your company was engaged in producing gas shells. At the two factories involved there was a strike by women workers, who were worried about the effects on their health of the substances used in the shells. The company's response to their concern was to sack them all and replace them'.

'I know nothing of that', Bailey said, stiffly.

Maddox intervened to protect his witness. 'Mr Tyroll has commented on what he characterised as my "giving evidence". It appears that he is now doing the same. May we know the authority for the incident he has just cited?'

The chairman asked, 'Is there authority for that story, Mr Tyroll?' I lifted the sheaf of photocopies. 'I have here photocopies of stories appearing at the time in the *Times* newspaper and in the *Daily Telegraph*. I will, if you wish, submit them to the witness for him to read, or call as a witness the lady whose research revealed these matters. I was merely trying to shorten the historical part of this hearing'.

The chairman turned towards Bailey. 'Do you accept Mr Tyroll's information as genuine, Mr Bailey?'

'I have to, sir. It was well before I joined the company'.

That earned him a sympathetic chuckle from all three of the Tribunal.

'Will you, then, accept from me, that there was a further strike in the company in 1932, following a reduction in wages, and that was dealt with in the same way, namely by the dismissal of all the strikers?'

'If you say so', he admitted grudgingly.

'And that, following that incident, the company became a non-union company until after the Second World War, when a Labour government became embarrassed at giving defence contracts to a non-union firm and a union was formed within the company's works?'

'That may be true', he said, 'but if I could explain my remarks of yesterday . . .'

I cut him off. 'There is no need for you to explain why you sought to give a false impression to the Tribunal yesterday. Mr Bailey. I'm sure we can all think of one'.

'Mr Tyroll!' warned the chairman. 'What was your explanation, Mr Bailey?'

'In preparing for this case, I thought it helpful to outline a little of the company's history. Although I have worked in the company all my adult life, I felt it wise to do a little research. I re-read the company's official history'.

The chairman nodded, as if that explained everything.

'And was the official history typed on the word processor in your office, too?'

'Mr Tyroll!' snarled the chairman, and I apologised, but my crack had raised a chuckle in the back rows, so it was good for morale.

Time to change ground again. 'You told us, Mr Bailey, that you had spent all your adult life working for BDS, is that so?'

'Yes', he said, 'It is'.

I nodded. 'And for much of that time you will have been a member of management, yes?'

'Well, for some years, yes'

I picked up a book from my table, 'So you will be fully familiar with the so-called Joint Agreement made between your firm and the Union in 1950 and amended in 1973 and 1982?'

'I am aware of it, of course. I don't know that I can claim to be fully familiar with it. It's a long document. I wouldn't pretend to know every detail of it'.

I nodded again. 'Can you just explain, for the benefit of the Tribunal, the nature of the Joint Agreement, what it actually is?'

He cleared his throat. 'It's a wide-ranging agreement, governing working practices in the company and the company's relations with the Union'.

'And it has a section on discipline, I believe?'

'Yes, it does'.

Sheila got up and distributed photocopies to the witness and the clerk. Maddox waved his away and produced a copy of the book from the papers on his table.

'These', I said, 'are copies of the

Agreement's section on discipline, which starts at Page 110 of the book. I take it you will accept that they are genuine copies?'

Bailey looked at Maddox, who nodded.

I asked for the document to be exhibited, and went on, 'You will see that Section B, on Page 112, is headed "Dismissal". Would you be good enough to read the opening paragraph, Mr Bailey?'

He glowered at me suspiciously, and began. '"In cases of serious industrial misconduct, e.g. violence, dishonesty, drunkenness etc, immediate dismissal may be deemed appropriate. If a question of immediate dismissal arises, the following procedure shall be followed..."'

I stopped him there. 'Now', I said, 'there follow a number of lettered paragraphs setting out the agreed procedure. Paragraph A says that the employee shall be informed of the proposal to dismiss him by written notice, setting out the reason or reasons for his dismissal. Is that right?'

He scanned the copy briefly. 'Yes', he said, 'it is. But if you're suggesting that I broke the procedure, it is obvious that I didn't. The letters of dismissal set out the reasons'.

'Apart', I reminded him, 'from Mr Afsar's, where your word processor accused him of an assault when he was not even there. However, it was the word "proposal" that I was interested in. What does that suggest to you?'

'I don't know. Immediate dismissal is immediate dismissal'.

'Well, let us look at Paragraph B, which says that "Any employee aggrieved by a decision to dismiss him or her immediately shall have a right to appeal against the decision to dismiss, provided that notice of appeal is given in writing to the Personnel Manager within fourteen days of the letter of dismissal". It goes on to say that "Notification of this right and the deadline shall be included in the letter of dismissal". Is that correct, Mr Bailey?'

This time he didn't even glance at his copy. 'Yes', he snapped. 'But I think in all the circumstances . . .'

I moved in quickly 'All *what* circumstances, Mr Bailey?'

'That I was exasperated. I had a major strike on my hands caused entirely by these people and I had just been assaulted'.

'You were, in fact, very angry, were you not? If what you say is true, that's quite understandable'.

'Yes. I was very angry'.

He wasn't far from very angry again, his pale face having darkened considerably.

'What', I enquired, 'makes you believe that your exasperation and anger override the Joint Agreement, Mr Bailey?'

He turned towards the Tribunal for support. 'I'm sure you will understand the pressures on me at that time and the anger I felt at being assaulted on the company's premises. I was not in the mood for following the letter of procedures'.

I nodded, sympathetically. 'So you say, and I'm sure the Tribunal will know how to assess the importance of your mood against the procedure laid down by an agreement between your company and the Union'.

Maddox had been looking at his watch every few seconds, in the hope of bringing relief to his beleaguered witness. It worked at last; the chairman looked at his and called the lunch adjournment. As I left the room I glanced at the press table. There was nobody there. No headlines for me.

CHAPTER TWENTY-EIGHT

It was difficult to get to the lift. Not only did Mulvaney, Martin and Afsar want to congratulate me, but also some of the lads from the public seats. I seemed to have convinced them they were getting their money's worth.

'Good stuff!' said Mulvaney, clapping me on the shoulder.

'Good enough', I agreed, 'but it's easy when they're batting. Wait till you're giving evidence and Maddox does it to you. Apart from which, we still haven't got round the fact that you called an illegal strike'.

Sheila and I retreated to the Cathedral churchyard again, while Con and the boys went off to celebrate Bailey's discomfiture. I hoped that Bailey was drinking deeply somewhere.

My hopes were rewarded by Bailey's complexion when we reassembled. Its pallor had turned pink with the flush of alcohol taken too quickly.

'Mr Bailey', I began, 'if I may return to the dismissal procedure in the Joint Agreement, what you seem to have said is that you were in such a mood at the time that you never even considered the provisions of the Agreement. Is that correct?'

He wasn't drunk enough to fall right into that. He paused for a while, then said, 'I was stressed and angry and I was in pain from the assaults inflicted by your clients'.

'So much so', I said, 'that you also failed to consider the Human Rights Act, am I right?'

He stared at me, genuinely nonplussed. 'I don't know anything about the Human Rights Act', he said at last.

Excellent answer. I left it there and changed tack.

'You told us, yesterday, about a period when BDS was plagued by wildcat strikes. You implied that the Union was not involved. Is that right?'

'Yes', he said. 'They were illegal and

unsupported strikes, brought about by people on the shop floor'.

'So, since they were illegal, you could have sought legal remedies against the strikers, you could have sought injunctions against them'.

'I could, yes, but they were too short, a day or two at most'.

I nodded. There was another question—one which had exercised my mind since I first understood the case—but there was no way that I was going to ask it.

'Was Mr Mulvaney employed by BDS at that time?'

'No', he grudgingly agreed.

'Or Mr Martin?'

'No', even more grudgingly.

'But there was a Union branch at the works?'

'Yes. I've told you, the Union didn't support any of those actions'.

'And who was the Union's representative at that time?'

'A Mr Dunn'.

'Is that the same Mr Dunn who was the firm's Personnel Manager at the same time?'

He stared at me with real dislike. 'As a matter of fact, yes. There was no reason why he should not be, and no one else put up for the post'.

'And do you think that the wildcat strikes may have arisen from a perception by the Union's members that their employers had in place a tame Union representative who was high on the firm's payroll?'

He clenched his fists. 'If you're implying what I think . . .' he began.

I cut him off. 'I'm implying nothing, and you need not bother to answer that question'.

Time to ease off, ready for the final scene.

'In your letters of dismissal, you accused all three of my clients of trespass, including the one who wasn't even at the gate. Is that a genuine complaint, or was that, too, an invention of your word processor?'

He scowled, in unison with the chairman who growled, 'Mr Tyroll' and lifted a threatening pencil.

'When I approached the gate', Bailey said, 'Mulvaney and Martin were standing inside the gate, in conversation with Barlow, the gate Security Guard'.

'They were talking to him?'

'Yes'.

'Do you know what they were talking about?'

'Barlow later confirmed to me that he was telling them that he had been instructed to exclude them and urging them to go away'.

'And you believed him?'

'Of course I believed him! Why should I not?'

I nodded. 'So, Mr Barlow was carrying out your instructions and, for all you knew, the Applicants were about to leave peacefully.

Yes?'

He snorted. 'For all I knew they might just as well have been about to walk further into the premises'.

'But they didn't?'

'Well, no, but that was because I arrived'.

'I see. And would you normally treat standing on the firm's premises as serious misconduct, warranting immediate dismissal?'

'Of course not. The letter is intended to refer to the trespass and the assaults together'.

I nodded again. 'And, while Mr Mulvaney and Mr Martin were standing innocently just inside your gate, you arrived', I said, evenly, 'and abused and attacked Mr Mulvaney'.

His black eyes widened and his flush deepened. 'I abused and attacked Mulvaney!' he exclaimed. 'I spoke to Mulvaney and he and Martin attacked me. I've told you that'.

'So you have, but like a lot of other things you have told the Tribunal, it is not true. The facts are, Mr Bailey, that you opened your office window and shouted something towards the gate when you first saw Mr Mulvaney and Mr Martin, and then you, Cheetham and Cantrell approached the gate. On your arrival, you abused Mr Mulvaney and struck him. He hit back in self-defence and you were restrained by Barlow and the others. Is that not what really happened?'

'I struck Mulvaney! Why on earth would I do that?'

'Because, Mr Bailey, you were stressed and angry, as you have said, and because you were also drunk'.

'I was drunk?' he almost shouted. 'Who says so?'

'Mr Tyroll!' snapped the chairman, 'I hope you are cross-examining on evidence and not merely attacking Mr Bailey'.

'Far be it from me, sir, to make a personal attack upon Mr Bailey', I said. I turned back to the witness. 'There are witnesses who will say that, when you attacked Mr Mulvaney you smelled strongly of alcohol . . .'

He half rose from his seat—as fine a picture of an aggressive drunk as one might wish—and cut me short. 'Witnesses!' he exclaimed. 'What witnesses?'

'You have fallen', I said, 'into a peculiar pattern of asking me questions, Mr Bailey, which is not the way it is supposed to work. You will hear the witnesses in due course'.

'They're liars!' he said.

'So far', I said, 'the only untruths which this Tribunal has heard have come from you, Mr Bailey', and I sat down.

The chairman called a surprise teabreak, presumably to give Bailey the chance to simmer down. Bailey used it to give Maddox an earbashing in the corridor about the way I had treated him. Now I knew why the Deputy Head of their legal section was presenting the case—Maddox's boss had won the toss.

Our audience were warmly enthusiastic about the cross-examination of Bailey, so I had to remind them again that this was the easy bit and hold up to Mulvaney the dangers of losing your temper while giving evidence.

The rest of the afternoon was filled with Greene and Swan. There were few surprises, although Greene recalled that it had been Bailey's idea to use computer personnel in Accounts and had even suggested Mohammed Afsar. I made a note to ask Mohammed if he had ever fallen out with Bailey previously. Had he been set up to be dismissed?

If he had, the answer might lie in what Swan said. He agreed that it was a regular practice, when work was slow in his section, for Accounts to borrow personnel. Nobody had ever refused before Mohammed, but Mohammed had been extremely critical of the practice and had said he would not co-operate. I pursued the point briefly.

'You say that you were aware that Mr Afsar objected to the practice, Mr Swan?'

'Yes', he agreed.

'Did you understand his objections?'

'I understood that a highly-trained computer programmer would not like to be used as mere input clerk, yes'.

'But you passed on Mr Greene's request, nevertheless?'

'I had no alternative. It was done with Mr Bailey's authority. I had to pass it on to

Mohammed'.

He was only obeying orders, even though he knew the terms of Mohammed's contract.

'As his Head of Section, you were aware of the detailed provisions of Mr Afsar's Contract of Employment? The job description?'

'Yes', he said and I sat down again.

'Bonzer!' said Sheila as she drove me home. 'You're not bad at this legal stuff, Chris Tyroll'.

She had seen me a couple of times in a Magistrates' Court, but this was the first time she had sat through a long cross-examination.

'Kind of you to say so', I said, 'but I'm not sure that we've got very far'.

'You've made Bailey a liar'.

'That would be good if we had a Jury or a bench of lay Magistrates, but those three on the Tribunal are professionals—barrister chairman, management representative and that dozy old berk from a union, who's only there for the fees and isn't paying attention anyway'.

'So you don't think you've done much good?'

'Well, I've cleared Mohammed of assault and trespass, I've minimised the trespass so that it can hardly be said to be worth instant dismissal and I've raised the shadow of serious breaches of the Joint Agreement'.

'So, it's not all bad, then. Who do we kick off with tomorrow?'

'Cheetham , I said. 'Because he was at the

gate, and Maddox and Bailey will be rehearsing him all night if necessary'.

I didn't need to prepare for Cheetham's evidence, so we relaxed and took an early night.

At two in the morning the phone rang. I came out of sleep cursing. I had done a deal with my assistant Alisdair that he would field all late night emergencies while the Tribunal hearing went on.

It was Alisdair calling. 'Sorry to drag you out, gaffer', he said, 'but John Parry's been on the emergency number'.

'Don't tell me', I said, 'he's been arrested'.

'No', he said, ignoring my sarcasm, 'he's got a suspicious death that he wants to talk to you about. I told him I'd try and contact you'.

'Thanks a million', I muttered. 'What's it about? Who's dead?'

'I don't know. Someone at Kerren Wood, I think. He's at the Police Station there. Will you ring him?'

I agreed and rang off. Sheila was sitting up. 'What's the go?' she enquired.

'John Parry's got himself a dead body and thinks I can help', I said and dialled Kerren Wood Police Station.

The switchboard put me through to John Parry. 'DI Parry', he answered, brusquely.

'Chris Tyroll', I said. 'This had better be good, to wake me at two when I've got a hearing in the morning. Who's dead?'

'Hello, Chris. I'd forgotten you've still got your Tribunal hearing, sorry. But I've got a dodgy death and I think you knew him. His wife says you did some business for him'.

'Who was he?'

'A bloke called Samson, lived in Kerren Wood'.

I had been coming more awake and that finally did it. 'Samson!' I exclaimed. 'How did he get himself killed?'

'A bit complicated and a bit peculiar', John said, 'but it looks like murder. Can you think of anyone who'd kill him?'

'Not at all', I said. 'What I did for him wasn't that kind of business—not the kind people kill over'.

'What time you going to the Tribunal tomorrow?' he asked.

'About nine'.

'Put an extra breakfast on. I'll see you in the morning when I've wrapped up here'. I suppose he was being kind and expected me to sleep after that, which of course I didn't. I lay and fretted about how a completely ordinary bloke like Samson had got himself murdered. Sheila, when I couldn't give her all the details, rolled over and went straight back to sleep. I fell asleep eventually, and dreamed of Sheila and I herding ponies and kangaroos across a great plain, which meant I woke up remembering that she was due back in Australia after Christmas.

CHAPTER TWENTY-NINE

John Parry and I sat either side of the breakfast table, his broad face pale from his long night on the case and me feeling like he looked. It seemed only decent to let him get some food and coffee in him before pressing him for details.

When I had woken up a little and he had relaxed, I asked about Samson. 'How did you know him?' he responded.

I told him about Maiden's pony-rustling and the way it all ended. 'I thought it was one of my better legal strokes', I said.

He nodded. 'Certainly doesn't look like the reason he was killed', he commented.

'You didn't seem entirely certain that it was murder last night', I said.

'No', he said, 'no, I wasn't, and I'm still not. It could have been an accident, but I don't think so'.

For some reason Sean McBride's death flickered at the back of my memory. 'What happened?' I asked.

'You know where he lived? In Kerren Wood?'

'Yes. He lived in one of those houses on the other side of the village, past the White Lion'.

'Right', said John. 'The White Lion was his local and that's where he'd been last night. He used to walk along the lane past the houses to the pub. Last night, as he was walking home, about 11.30, he was hit by a car and left dead at the roadside'.

'It's a bit of a dodgy lane and 11.30 is premium time for drunken drivers. Surely it's just a hit and run?'

He poured himself another coffee. 'I don't think so. We've got a witness who has a strange story'.

'A witness who saw the impact?' I said.

He shook his head. 'No, no. Not that good, but good nevertheless. You know the grass track that opens on the left, about halfway between the White Lion and the end of the houses?'

'Yes. It used to be the access to an old Coal Board tipping site, but now it's just a lovers' lane'.

'Well', he said, 'right opposite that opening lives Mr Arthur Freeman. Mr Freeman is old and lives alone and disapproves of almost everything, including television, which he does not watch very much'.

'Is this going somewhere?' I asked, impatiently.

'Hold hard, boyo, and all will be revealed. Last evening, Arthur Davies was enjoying one of his favourite occupations, namely sitting in his front room keeping a disapproving eye on the narrow world of Kerren Wood, like Captain Cat himself only a good deal less kindly'.

'He's not blind like Captain Cat, is he?' I asked.

'No, no. Far from it. Anyway, he saw Samson pass by on his way to the White Lion at about eight. Then he saw a car come from the direction of the White Lion and back into the opening opposite his gaff'.

'Fornicators?' I hazarded.

'Well, of course, that's what he thought and that's one of his favourite gripes. They park in there, he told me, and when they get down to business they bang bits of themselves on the horn button or their alarms go off by accident. Apart from the sinfulness, he objects to the noise. Says that sometimes he's gone across and banged on the car windows and told them to go'.

'Sounds a really nice old person', I said, remembering my own days of gymnastics in a Mini. If some old voyeur had come and banged on my window at the wrong moment I'd have died.

'Yes, well, you have to take the witnesses you've got in my business. It's not like being a lawyer, where you can bribe them and rehearse them and . . .'

'Shut up, or tell me the rest', I said. 'Did he go across for a closer view last night?'

'No. He didn't because it wasn't a courting couple and there wasn't any noise. It was a man in the car—on his own'.

'And what did he do? The man in the car?'

'That's what intrigued old Arthur. He thought it must be an assignation with some local woman, so he sat and watched to see which of his neighbours' wives or daughters was up to something and was going to turn up and join the bloke in the car'.

'And who did?'

'Nobody. The bloke just sat in his motor—Davies says he thinks the bloke was reading a book—and nobody else came along'.

'That's odd!' I said.

'Isn't it just? Why would you park in a lovers' lane on your own on a September evening and sit there for nearly three hours, maybe reading a book?'

Sheila had been sitting silent. Now she joined in. 'Perhaps he's an incurable romantic whose greatest moments were in that lane and he comes back on the anniversaries and gives himself a Sherman for old times' sake'.

'A Sherman?' queried John.

'A wank', she explained.

'It's J. Arthur in English', he said, severely. 'And that wasn't what he was doing. He was waiting for Samson'.

'How do you know?'

'Because, about 11.30, he switched on his lights and shot out of the entry in the direction of the White Lion'.

'How does that prove he hit Samson?' asked Sheila.

'It doesn't. What proves it is the man who found Samson. He was another drinker from the White Lion. He came down the road just after a car had gone the other way. He found Samson lying at the roadside and went to the phone. Old Arthur saw him go to the phone box just past the lovers' lane entrance'.

'Still doesn't make it deliberate', I objected. 'Whatever the bloke in the car was doing in the lane, he still might have hit Samson by accident'.

John shook his head. 'Where Samson was found there's a footpath, separated from the roadway by a little strip of grass. It runs all the way from the village, past the White Lion and past the houses. He'd been walking on that and whoever hit him went right off the road, across the grass, onto the footpath, hit Samson and turned back onto the road, disappearing towards Belston. It's clear from the tyre marks'.

'Didn't anyone at the White Lion see anything?'

'No. You can't see the point of impact from the car park. There were still a couple of blokes in the car park and they saw a car flash by, but they didn't pay it much mind'.

'But old Arthur can describe the car? And the driver?'

John shook his head, glumly. 'Old Arthur regards motor cars as instruments of the Devil, made for mobile fornication. He can't tell a

Rolls from a Volkswagen. As to the driver—all he knows is that it was a bloke'.

'Is he sure of that?'

'Oh yes. Apparently the guy had his interior light on for a minute or two after he pulled into the lane, so Arthur saw him'.

'Description?'

'Tall, with short hair, maybe brown. That's all'.

'Well, the short hair is probably true. With Arthur's preoccupation, people who do wicked things probably have long hair, so I doubt he's invented that. And that's all?'

'That's all. We're getting some clear tyre prints identified, and now it's light my boys'll be searching the scene for paint scrapes or whatever, but we haven't got much. Haven't you got any ideas?'

'Nope', I said. 'I can't say that I knew much about Samson, but he struck me as a fairly ordinary sort of bloke. If you ask me, the most extraordinary thing that ever happened to him was having his daughter's pony rustled by Dennis Maiden, and that didn't get him killed'. I turned out to be wrong about the last bit.

I looked at my watch. 'I've got a Tribunal to charm in Brum, I said. 'This facility is closing until this evening. Let us know how you go'.

226

CHAPTER THIRTY

Reg Cheetham, I thought, was there to confirm Bailey's version of the assaults at the gate, but Maddox had him give other evidence as well. Cheetham had been a member of the Union, and was able to describe the meeting at which Mulvaney had reported on the firm's treatment of Mohammed. I expected him to say that Con had not just suggested a strike ballot but had urged it. I was wrong. According to Cheetham, Con had made his report of Mohammed's situation and called for debate. It was Jimmy Martin who had put the motion to strike and argued for it vigorously. As expected, his account of the fracas at the gate was a perfect match for Bailey's version, even to the extent that Maddox had to warn him off dragging Mohammed back into it and explain that it "had been agreed" that Mohammed was not present. Cheetham seemed suitably shocked by the assaults he claimed to have witnessed, and Maddox believing he had considerably bolstered his boss's case.

Cheetham was never going to admit to me that he was lying. He might crack a bit under cross-examination, but basically he would cling to his story and the more I pressed him the more he would repeat the bare details. I needed to approach him from a different direction.

'Mr Cheetham', I began, 'you told us that you were in Mr Bailey's office just before the incident at the gate, and that it was you that saw Mr Mulvaney and Mr Martin talking to the Gate Security Officer, is that so?'

'That's right. Mr Cantrell had just phoned the gate and told Barlow to keep them out and a minute or two later I happened to glance out of the window and saw them'.

'And did you know why they were there?'

'No. I had no idea'.

'You had no idea', I repeated. 'You were at the Union meeting when the strike ballot was voted for?'

'Yes'.

'And were you at the meeting later, when Mr Mulvaney gave details of how the strike would be conducted?'

He glanced around nervously. He wanted to deny it, but he knew there were people at the back of the room who would have seen him. 'Well, yes, I was'.

'Do you recall what Mr Mulvaney said?'

'He gave us the day of the strike and said that it must be done in an orderly fashion'.

'What did he mean by that?'

'Well, he said that, in the past there had been wildcat strikes and the company had accused the strikers of sabotage. He said that this was a legitimate strike and that he was not going to give BDS any excuse for any such accusation'.

I nodded. 'So what did he instruct people to do?'

'He said we were not to just stay away from work, that we were to clock on as usual and see what work was in our section. If there were incomplete operations in the section that might be damaged by being left unfinished, we were to work on until they were done and safe. Then we could leave'.

'He said more, didn't he?'

Cheetham was not a happy man, but he answered at last. 'Yes, he said that he and the Shop Stewards would supervise the close down of each section'.

I nodded again. 'Now, we know that you did not obey the call to strike, despite your presence at the relevant meetings, so I imagine that you told Mr Bailey what had been said at those meetings'.

'Well, yes, I did'.

There was a low muttering along the back rows and the chairman glared at them.

'So', I said, 'it was simply not true that neither you nor Mr Bailey knew why they were there when you saw my clients at the gate?'

Cheetham flung an apologetic glance at Bailey and said, 'Well, I did tell Mr Bailey that they must be there to see the next section close down'.

'Now, you haven't told us how your day started that morning, Mr Cheetham, have you?'

He looked surprised. 'How my day started? I don't know what you mean'.

'I mean, what time did you get to work? What time did you clock on?'

His dignity affronted, he said, 'I don't clock on. I sign in at the General Office'.

It had served to rattle him a bit more. 'So, what time did you sign in?'

'Just before half past eight'.

'What did you do then?'

'I went straight to my section'.

'Now, Mr Cheetham, you've told us all about the way Mr Mulvaney had set out how the strike should begin, about his anxiety that there should be no wasted product or materials. What was the state of play in your section at the beginning of that morning?'

'There were, there was, there was work not completed by the night shift'.

The chairman intervened. 'Mr Tyroll, if you are going to ask this witness about the process in his section, I shall have to stop you. We are dealing with matters that are covered by the Official Secrets Act'.

For all I knew Cheetham's section might be responsible for the supply of toast to the Canteen, but once the Official Secrets Act has been waved over something it doesn't exist any more. So I nodded and smiled.

'Thank you, Mr Chairman. It is not the nation's secrets I am concerned with, only Mr

Cheetham's own secrets'.

The chairman didn't understand me, but Cheetham did and I saw the flicker of shock in his eyes.

'So, you knew your section would work on to completion and that would be about mid-morning, yes?'

'Yes'.

'And just before that time you were in Mr Bailey's office?'

'Yes'.

'Why was that?'

'He had sent for me. He sent Mr Cantrell for me'.

'I see. Might I ask what was the matter that was so important that Mr Bailey was giving it his attention in the early hours of the strike?'

'I don't think I can answer that. It was a confidential matter'.

'Do you mean confidential as in Official Secrets Act, or confidential as in you don't want to tell me'.

'It was a confidential personnel matter. I don't think I can tell you'.

'It concerned a member of your section?' I asked.

He saw a way out. 'Yes', he said quickly. 'It was a disciplinary matter', and he glanced again at Bailey.

'A disciplinary matter so important that Mr Bailey chose to deal with it while most of the workforce were waltzing off', I said. 'Was that because it involved you—yourself?'

If he denied it I was stymied, because I couldn't prove the rumour that Con had from the men in Cheetham's section, but I hoped I had made him nervous enough.

'Alright!' he exclaimed. 'I suppose you think it's funny. It was to do with me. When Mr Cantrell came looking for me I was in the Rest Room. I was playing cards'.

A ripple of chuckles ran along the audience behind us and the chairman glowered again. Cheetham slouched down in his chair and Bailey stared hard at him.

'But you still have your job?' I said.

'I have made a full apology to Mr Bailey, and he has forgiven me', Cheetham asserted with the fervour of one saved from the burning.

'At the gate', I continued, 'you have told us what you recall, but that is not true, is it? The fact is that Mr Bailey abused and struck Mr Mulvaney without provocation and that Mr Mulvaney retaliated in self-defence, isn't it?'

'No. It isn't! It happened just the way I described'.

'Mr Cheetham', I said, 'I don't see much point in taking this much further. You have told us that you were a member of the Union, but you ignored the call to strike and relayed the Union's affairs to Mr Bailey. When Mr Cantrell caught you loafing on the firm's time, you were forgiven by Mr Bailey and you now support his version of events at the gate. Thank you', and I sat down.

CHAPTER THIRTY-ONE

If Cheetham had been one of the company's finks in the Union, there was a bigger one close behind. The Respondents' next witness was none other than Harry Goatly, Midland Area Secretary of the Union.

He was a thin, long-faced man of about forty, with a pockmarked face, mousy curls and horn-rimmed spectacles. Sheila hissed, 'Why would I recognise him?'

'Dunno', I answered, my mind elsewhere.

Offhand I couldn't think of any occasion when I'd even heard of a union officer giving evidence for an employer in an Employment Tribunal. That Goatly was prepared to stick his neck out so far made it clear that he and BDS were bosom pals. I wondered what his reward would be.

His purpose here was plain—it was to fire the heavy shots that would sink Con Mulvaney's case by establishing that his strike was unofficial and illegal.

Maddox led his witness through a brief personal history. He was not a man who had come up in the ranks of the Union, but a professional full-time officer who had come to his present post from—surprise, surprise—a government administrative association. He had been Midland Secretary for five years.

He told us that he was fully familiar with the Union's Rules and Procedure book, somehow contriving to give the impression that it was his daily study and that he never left home without it. Maddox asked him about strike procedure.

'We would never begin by considering withdrawal of labour', he said, prissily. 'That is a last option. At every stage we would seek to negotiate a compromise'.

Maddox smiled at him, approvingly. 'Perhaps', he invited, 'you would take us through the stages of what did happen at BDS and what should have happened according to the agreed procedures and the rules of your Union?'

Goatly was more than willing and settled himself in his chair. 'I understand', he began, 'that you have heard about the incident when Mohammed Afsar refused to obey an order of Mr Bailey's. Well, following that, I believe that there was a meeting between Mr Bailey and Con Mulvaney, the Chairman of Shop Stewards, but they were unable to resolve the problem'.

'Why do you imagine that was?'

'Well, I wasn't there, but Mr Mulvaney can be a difficult man to deal with and unwilling to give way . . .'

I rose. 'Sir, I accept that this Tribunal can admit hearsay evidence, but this is not hearsay, this is a witness who doesn't know what happened because he wasn't there and he hasn't even been told and my friend is inviting him to *imagine* what occurred'.

To my surprise the chairman agreed. 'Mr Maddox', he said, 'I really do not think that the witness's imagination will take us anywhere useful. Can we try and proceed on the facts?'

Maddox grovelled and turned back to his witness. 'Whatever the cause, the problem was not resolved between Mr Bailey and Mulvaney?'

'No. Mulvaney and others then visited Mr Capstick, our National Secretary'.

'And what was his advice?'

'He told Mulvaney that he had a bee in his bonnet about undermanning, that these were difficult times and BDS must be given latitude to manage their business. He also asked me to look into the matter'.

'Which you did?'

'Oh, yes. At the first opportunity I met with Mr Bailey and we reached a compromise'.

'Which was?'

'That Mr Afsar would be reinstated without even having to apologise'.

'And you, as the Union's appointed representative, believed that to be fully satisfactory?'

Goatly nodded. 'Of course'.

'And what did Mr Mulvaney say when you told him?'

'He said that it was acceptable so long as Mr Afsar's pension and redundancy rights were protected. I told him that we had not even discussed that and he must trust Mr Bailey'.

'And how did he react?'

'He was very angry and said that he'd take it to a meeting of the Branch'.

Maddox then led Goatly through the run-up to the strike, getting him to emphasise the fact that only Capstick had the authority to issue the ballot or the notice of strike.

Finally he asked, 'As a full-time Union officer, it is unusual to see you giving evidence for an employer. Might I ask why that is?'

'Certainly. I am here because I believe that I must protect the jobs of my members and that the strike which Mulvaney called threatened those jobs'.

Maddox smiled and sat down.

There's an old legal maxim—'When the answer's a lemon, make lemonade'. I've always taken it to mean that, when you can't get the evidence you want, do the best you can with the evidence you've got. So I stood up to try.

People use words differently. You probably use them to convey information; people like me use them to persuade; bureaucrats like Goatly use them to conceal information. Imbued with the old bureaucratic belief that you must never be responsible for a decision, they use words to obscure what they're actually saying, so that they can always deny it. So—no point in fencing much with Mr Goatly. Just go in quick, do what you can and get out quick.

'I'm glad', I began, 'that you're here to protect your members' jobs. That's why I'm here, to protect the jobs of three of your members. I'm glad for another reason. It has been in my mind to call you for the Applicants, as there are one or two matters that you can explain. However, let's leave them till later. You have told us about Mr Mulvaney's reaction to your deal with Mr Bailey, when he said he would take it to a Branch Meeting. Were you present at that meeting?'

'No', he said, shortly.

'That meeting voted, by an overwhelming majority, to ballot for a strike, and such a ballot was conducted. Did you have any hand in that?'

'Certainly not. I've told you that . . .'

I stopped him. 'Were you present at the meeting where Mr Mulvaney gave advice to the Branch as to how the strike should be conducted?'

'No'.

'Were you present at BDS when the strike commenced?'

'No. I had telephone conversations with Mr Bailey and, eventually, I came to see him when the strike spread to Coventry'.

'So, you do not know, of your own

knowledge, what representations were made to the members at Belston which led them to vote for a strike?'

'No, but I know that the ballot was illegal and the Union couldn't and didn't support the strike. When Mr Bailey informed us of the notice Mr Capstick wrote and withdrew it'.

I should have cut that answer short after the first syllable, but I nodded. 'You have told us about your knowledge of the Union's rules, procedures and practices', I said, picking up the Rules. 'Do you recall this piece about the "Duties of Branch Officers"?' and I read him the piece to which Con had referred me:

' "Once elected, Branch Officers are subject in the first place to the wishes of the Membership of their Branch as expressed by a majority vote of a General Meeting of the Branch" '.

'That doesn't over-ride the authority of the National Secretary', he snapped.

'No', I agreed, 'but the National Secretary's authority is similarly derived from a majority of a national General Meeting. Was there such a meeting about the Belston strike?'

'No', he agreed, reluctantly.

'When you made your agreement with Mr Bailey, about Mohammed Afsar, did you take into account that Mr Bailey had broken the disciplinary rules in the Joint Agreement?'

'We weren't concerned with rules then. We were trying to find a reasonable solution to the dispute'.

'Ah!' I exclaimed, 'I see. When Management loses its temper and sacks someone, the rules don't matter, but when a Shop Steward pays too strict attention to the rules, that's illegal. Is that it?' Cheap shot, but it pleased the public seats.

'No, but . . .'

I cut him off and changed direction. 'When you met with Mr Bailey about the spread of the strike to Coventry, what was the purpose of that meeting?'

'I wanted to assist BDS in ending the strike—at Coventry and at Belston'.

'You wanted to assist BDS, I see. And how did you do that?'

'Well, Mr Bailey intended to publish a statement to all the workers at Coventry, telling them the truth about the Belston strike. I was able to assist him with that and to see that the Union's image was not damaged by anything he said'.

I turned to Maddox and asked if he had, by any chance, a copy of that statement. He produced one and I asked him to pass it to Goatly. Taking another document from my own file, I turned back to the witness.

'Is that Mr Bailey's message to the Coventry workforce?'

'Yes, it is'.

'And does it begin like this—"The present strike at Coventry has been mis-represented as a legitimate dispute about an alleged policy of undermanning by BDS and, in particular, about the so-called victimisation of a Computer Operator. Neither of these allegations are true and the strike is clearly illegal"?'

'Yes', he said.

'Good, and is it headed with the address of BDS at Belston?'

'Yes'.

'And is it marked "Confidential" at the top?'

'No', he said, puzzled. 'It's marked "To all workers at our Coventry Branch"'

'Do you know why mine is different, Mr Goatly?'

He shook his head, still looking puzzled. 'No', he said.

'It may be because the document from which I read—which is word-for-word identical in its text to the document you hold—is not Mr Bailey's circular to the Coventry workers, but a confidential report by you to Mr Capstick, sent three weeks before the Coventry strike as your view of the Belston strike. Have a look!' and I passed him the papers. 'Is that not your report?'

He sat with a document in each hand. He barely glanced at the second; he knew it was his. Glaring at me sullenly he finally managed a 'Yes'.

Lemonade, maybe, but it still had a lump in it which I couldn't see the Tribunal swallowing.

I asked for both documents to be exhibited for the Applicants and sat down. As I turned back to my place I noted that one of the reporters was at the back. Walters wasn't there, but some paper would be able to report that a senior official of the Union had sworn that the strike was illegal.

The next day was a waste of time. Maddox called a succession of witnesses who were all members of the Union who had not gone on strike. Each one was there to say that Jimmy Martin had been the prime mover of the proposition to ballot for a strike. None of them, curiously, could recall who seconded Jimmy's motion, but apart from that they were hardly worth cross-examination. With the last one Maddox closed his case and we adjourned till the next day.

We gathered in a cafe along the street, Sheila and I, my clients and a selection of their supporters. The fans were jubilant and, again, I had to calm them down. I didn't tell them that it had gone a lot better than I had expected.

'Look', I said, 'we've made some progress. We've established that the sacking of Mohammed was in breach of the Joint Agreement and that even Bailey won't argue that trespass is a reason for dismissal. We've established that Mohammed wasn't part of the incident at the gate, so maybe he's in the clear, but we've still got the calling of the strike and the scuffle at the gate'.

'Nobody will believe Cheetham now', someone said.

'You made an absolute galah out of him', Sheila agreed.

'Maybe', I said, 'but those three on the Tribunal can pick and choose who they believe, and they may well choose to believe Cheetham, despite the fact that he's in hock to Bailey for his job, added to which, we've had Goatly telling them that, even according to the Union, the strike was illegal'.

'Then why did they let it run three weeks, instead of going for an injunction?' Martin asked.

'You tell me', I said. 'I have to say that the High Court would have given BDS an injunction against you like a shot on this evidence'.

I repeated the advice I had been giving my clients for weeks about their own behaviour when giving evidence and our meeting broke up. A case is never so strong as when your opponent has just finished giving evidence, but tomorrow we had to put on our own show.

CHAPTER THIRTY-TWO

There were no reporters at the hearing next morning, and one of the Tribunal was late arriving, so we waited a while. I took the opportunity to play lawyers' games with Maddox.

'You know', I told him, 'it's not too late. You could still make us a sensible offer'.

'An offer!' he said. 'What for? We're winning'.

I smiled. 'You're not going to win against Mohammed. He was improperly sacked and any assault by him has gone out the window. You aren't arguing trespass as a reason for dismissal. All you've got is the strike and the brawl at the gate'.

'All!' he exclaimed. 'It's more than enough'.

'Ah, but at what a price!' I said. 'Your boss being branded as a drunk who's fast with his fists. Even if you win, he'll be known as "Basher Bailey" ever after'.

The thought made him stare at me for a moment, then he shook his head.

'You're just playing games', he said. 'All you trial lawyers are the same—no evidence, just bluff and tricks'.

'You don't usually do trials?' I asked, knowing full well that he didn't. He spent his time advising on how to break someone else's patents and get away with it.

He shook his head. 'Mr Bailey decided that we would handle this one in-house, that's all'.

'Why was that?' I enquired.

'To tell you the truth', he said, 'it was the Americans. We were just getting things nicely sorted out with them when we ran into difficulties because Coventry fell behind. They weren't happy about that, but the strike at Belston nearly put the tin hat on it. We had to show them we could deal with a wildcat strike, and we have to show them that we're not making a big thing of it. If we'd pulled some big QC in, the papers would have been all over it'.

'But the American deal is done?'

'Oh, yes. Signed, sealed and delivered. We just didn't want to worry them at all'.

'So, how come your boss isn't here?'

'He'd already booked his holidays', Maddox said sharply and I grinned inwardly. I was right—Maddox had lost the toss.

The Tribunal assembled at last and I got to call Mohammed. He was a perfect witness. He looked serious and thoughtful, listened to my questions and gave considered answers. It didn't take long for him to tell his story and then Maddox got his chance. I wasn't worried about that and I was right. He was probably the first witness that Maddox had cross-examined for years—maybe the first ever—and no harm came of it.

It's always nice to leave a cross-examiner something to shoot himself in the foot with. I had not referred to the terms of Mohammed's contract with BDS, but I'd primed Mohammed. When Maddox pressed him about the reasons for his refusal to go into

Accounts, Mohammed took his contract from his jacket pocket and started to read his job description from it. Maddox was silly enough not to stop him and after that it became an Exhibit.

All in all, Mohammed came across as a reasonable bloke who had objected to unreasonable treatment, but Maddox's cross-examination took so long we were well into the afternoon by the time he finished and the chairman decided to adjourn early for the weekend.

Sheila and I were hardly home before a car drew in outside and the doorbell rang. John Parry stood on the doorstep.

'Have you ever thought', I said as I opened the front door, 'that your life would be a lot more efficient if you moved in here?'

'Well, the cooking's an attraction and the landlady's a delight, but I doubt if I could afford the rent'.

'We could work something out. You could put your uniform on and stand at the gate bending the knees and saying, "Move along there!" now and then to keep burglars at bay. You have got a uniform, haven't you?'

'Course I have, boyo. Keep it all pressed in plastic bags, ready for when I get the Queen's Police Medal'.

I took him into the front room and gave him a drink then I went through to the kitchen and told Sheila to bung another fistful of witchetty grubs on.

'You haven't eaten?' I asked as I came back.

'No. When the forces of law and order are in hot pursuit of dangerous maniacs they pause not for rest nor refreshment, bach'.

'I take it you're here about Samson. Any news?'

'Yes', he said. 'The tyre tracks gave us a lead on the car and guess what? Samson was in the White Lion the night before with a bloke driving just such a car'.

'Did anyone know who he was?'

He shook his head. 'No, seems he was a total stranger. He turned up early in the evening and asked the barman if Samson was likely to be in. The barman told him Samson usually came in about eight, so the stranger waited. Barman says that Samson seemed quite surprised to see him when he came in, but the stranger bought him a drink, they had a bit of a chat and then our man made off'.

'Did Samson tell anyone who he was?'

'Apparently he said he'd done a bit of business with the bloke and he thought he was awkward about it, but he seemed pleasant enough now. He never said what the business was, though'.

'And you don't know who he was?'

'No, but we got some good descriptions. They notice strangers in Kerren Wood. That's why I'm here'.

He pulled a paper from his pocket. 'Have a

look at that. It's an E-Fit made up from five descriptions of Samson's drinking pal. Ever seen him?'

I took the picture. 'I doubt it', I said. 'I told you, I barely knew Samson, except as a client'.

I looked at the drawing. I thought I recognised it, but then, you always think that, don't you, whenever you see one of those made up pictures. I looked again and I still thought I recognised it.

Sheila came in to warn us for dinner and looked over my shoulder. 'I know him', she announced.

'Who is he, then?' asked John.

'He's that bloke you were talking to in the churchyard, Monday lunchtime, isn't he?'

So he was, or very nearly so.

I told John about meeting Samson in Birmingham. 'You never told me', he accused.

'You never asked. Anyway, we just ran into each other as he was crossing the Cathedral churchyard. Then he went off and this other bloke came along', and I tapped the paper.

'And who is he?'

'So far as I know he's a freelance reporter called Walters. He was in the Tribunal on the first morning. I imagine he operates in Brum. I've certainly never seen him hereabouts'.

John whipped out his mobile phone and called his office, giving Walters' name and setting his men trying to trace the reporter.

'Now then', he said, slipping the phone

away, 'what was this Walters fellow talking about?'

It came back—how Walters had asked if that was Samson I was talking to, and I told John.

'So he didn't know Samson?'

'Hang on a mo! He must have known Samson already, because he saw me talking to Samson and came up right afterwards and asked if it was Samson'.

John nodded. 'What did he say his interest in Samson was?'

'He said he'd done a story about Samson and his mate's ponies'.

'He didn't say who he wrote for? You're sure he's a reporter?'

'No and yes. At least, he was at the press table in the Tribunal on the first morning. He hasn't been back, though, but that's not surprising. There's not many reporters spend time in the Tribunals unless there's some juicy sexual harassment or a spot of racism or something'.

'And you've never seen Walters before?'

'Not so far as I know, no'.

'You, Chris Tyroll, are always a great help to my enquiries. You put a name to the face I'm looking for and then leave me with the question—why on earth would a Brummy journalist lie in wait for a saddler from Kerren Wood and kill him?'

'Perhaps the picture only looks like Walters.

Perhaps it's not him'.

He looked at me scornfully. 'The bloke in this picture waited for Samson at the White Lion. Your Mr Walters—who just happens to look like the bloke in this picture—talked to you about Samson and claimed to know him. Go on—tell me that's a coincidence, then!'

'Well, no. I wasn't going to say that'.

'Just as well', he declared. 'There is no such thing as coincidence except in badly constructed defences. Where's the grub, Sheila?'

CHAPTER THIRTY-THREE

John was right. We pushed the problem around over dinner and sat drinking and arguing about it afterwards, but it always came back to the same pattern. Walters saw Samson with me in Birmingham and checked with me to make sure of his identification. That night, a stranger who looked like Walters waited for Samson at the White Lion and bought him a drink. The following night someone driving the same kind of car as the stranger lay in wait for Samson and ran him down. You'd need a pretty flexible coincidence to wrap itself around all that lot.

Still—no amount of whisky, coffee or bright ideas produced a glimmer of a reason why

Walters should want to kill Samson. In the end, Sheila and I admitted defeat and left the problem to John and his merry men.

Monday morning we came back to the Tribunal. Automatically I looked for Walters at the press table as I walked in, but he wasn't there and he didn't show during the rest of the day.

The hearing resumed and I called Jimmy Martin. He seemed to be making a good impression as I took him through his recollection of events. On his part in the strike vote, he said that it was his considered opinion that BDS' policy of undermanning would only be stopped by strike action. He pointed out that everyone at the meeting had a mind of their own and that almost all of them had voted to strike, at the general meeting and in the ballot that followed. At the end, describing the fracas at the gate, he was quite cool and, I thought, believable, when he described Bailey's drunken rage, most particularly to anyone who had seen Bailey give evidence.

I sat down fairly well satisfied and Maddox got up.

'Mr Martin', he said, 'this story of Mr Bailey being drunk and assaulting Mulvaney is a pure fabrication, isn't it?'

Martin shook his head. 'No, it's not. You could smell it on him'.

Maddox ignored the answer. 'The reality is, isn't it, that you and Mulvaney resented being ordered from the company's premises and attacked a man much older than you?'

'And nearly twice my size!' Jimmy shot back.

The rear rows laughed and Maddox swivelled, adding his glare to the chairman's. I hoped that Jimmy wouldn't be tempted to play to the gallery.

'Mulvaney', stated Maddox, 'punched Mr Bailey in the face, and you took the opportunity to strike a blow from behind while Mr Bailey was being attacked by your comrade. Those are the facts, aren't they?'

Jimmy shook his head. 'The facts, Mr Maddox, are that Mr Bailey came across the yard bellowing like a raging bull. When he came up with us he gave Con Mulvaney a mouthful of abuse and then he hit him. Con hit back and Cantrell and Cheetham and I helped George Barlow stop Bailey before he hurt someone'. He was quite calm.

Maddox didn't have the sense to leave it alone. He dragged on for some time, repeating accusations at Jimmy, who fielded them all quietly and confidently. At last Bailey saw that they were doing no good and pulled Maddox down. I called Con Mulvaney

Con took his place at the witness table and sat back, unbuttoning his jacket. I had warned him that a man of his build would look lowering and aggressive if he leaned forward over the table, and I was glad to see that he'd remembered my advice, but he refused to be sworn on the New Testament and affirmed instead. I was sorry about that, because there is an old-fashioned prejudice against witnesses who won't be sworn.

Once again we went, step by step, through the run up to the strike. Con was the picture of a reasonable man faced with an unreasonable management and an unhelpful Union. He explained his contempt for wildcat strikers and his determination that there should be no accusations of sabotage, and gave an account of his battle with Bailey that agreed with Jimmy Martin's.

Maddox had learned his lesson with Jimmy. His cross-examination on the fight was perfunctory, as though it was only to be expected that Mulvaney would lie about it. Then he turned to the real weakness of Con's case—the setting up of the strike ballot.

'Your National Secretary, Mr Capstick, asked Mr Goatly to look into your complaints about Mr Afsar's dismissal, yes?'

'Yes'.

'And Mr Goatly is the Regional Secretary and, as I understand it, is superior to you in the Union's hierarchy?'

'Not superior, no. He is a salaried officer who chairs the Midland Council of the Union and is supposed to assist Midland branches'.

'I see. And in that capacity he came to Belston to assist you, yes?'

'He came to Belston when Mr Capstick told

him to', said Con.

'And he had a meeting with Mr Bailey at which you were not present, is that right?'

'Yes'.

'And afterwards he told you what had been agreed?'

'Yes'.

'And you disagreed?'

'Of course. Goatly had no authority from the Branch to make agreements in our name and he'd left Mohammed exposed to further problems and the firm's undermanning reinforced'.

'So you called a general meeting and told them to strike, yes?'

I rose. 'Mr Chairman, even the Respondent's witness Cheetham agrees that Mr Mulvaney did not advise a strike'.

Maddox apologised with a pained smile and continued. 'When the meeting voted to strike, you organised a ballot'.

'Yes. It's a legal requirement'.

'A legal requirement', Maddox repeated, 'Yet you did not have the authority of your Union to do so, did you?'

'I had all the authority I needed—the vote of a general meeting of my Branch. That's who I'm responsible to under the Union's Rules'.

'Mr Goatly has told us that you were in the wrong according to the Union's Rules, Mr Mulvaney. You may take it from me, and if I'm wrong I'm sure the Chairman will correct me, that you were also acting illegally when you set up the strike ballot and gave notice to Mr Bailey of a strike, weren't you?'

The chairman nodded his approval of that view. Con stared at Maddox for a moment, then said, 'I don't care what the law says. I had an obligation to my Branch members'.

Maddox smiled like a wolf. He had the answer he wanted and he could sit down. It was near the end of the day. The chairman checked his watch and muttered to his companions, then looked at me.

'Mr Tyroll', he said, 'We've heard all three of the Applicants. Can you tell us how many more witnesses you will be calling?'

So they were bored with listening to the Applicants' evidence and wanted to get it over. I rose.

'The issues are fairly clear in this matter, sir', I said, 'and we have heard from the Respondents' own witnesses about events at the various meetings before the strike. I think that all that matters now is the occurrence at the factory gate. I have one witness I intend to call as to that, sir'.

Maddox and Bailey were in hurried consultation, no doubt wondering who was our witness.

'Then we might finish the evidence tomorrow morning?' the chairman asked.

'That', I said, smiling warmly at Maddox, 'rather depends on how long my friend spends on his cross-examination'.

We adjourned, with Maddox and Bailey still muttering at each other. At least I had blunted Maddox's triumph over Con Mulvaney.

John Parry phoned that night. He wanted to know if I was sure that the reporter's name was Walters. It seemed that no one in Birmingham had heard of a freelance called Walters.

CHAPTER THIRTY-FOUR

George Barlow was my last witness. Somewhat to my surprise he had agreed readily to give us an account of what happened at the gate, and we could not have wanted a better witness.

He was the archetypal former copper—tall, solid, careful in his speech, and with steady eyes that took in everything around him. He took the witness' chair in his BDS Security uniform. Somewhere I read a piece of research that says that Courts believe a witness in uniform more readily than one in civvies—any uniform, Boy Scouts, commissionaires, bus drivers, whatever—so they ought to believe old George.

I took him through his years of service with the Staffordshire Police and the Central Midlands force, his two commendations and his rank of sergeant at retirement, then his employment at BDS.

I knew that his appearance here would be surprising to the Tribunal and I asked him about the new contract arrangements for security at BDS.

'Yes, sir', he said. 'I understand that, in the light of the American Retaliator contract, it was decided to extend security and a contract firm is in the process of taking over'.

'So, at present, you work under Mr Cantrell, the contractor's manager?'

'That's correct, sir'.

'You don't object to the new arrangements, Mr Barlow?'

'No, sir. The company is entitled to make any arrangements it thinks necessary for security and, anyway, the new arrangements won't affect me very much. I am due to retire shortly'.

I nodded. 'So you're not here to give evidence out of any resentment against BDS?'

The chairman interrupted. 'Mr Tyroll! This is your own witness! You are not cross-examining him, are you?'

'No, sir. I am seeking to establish Mr Barlow's credentials as an independent witness, sir'.

The chairman nodded, suspiciously, and I signed to George to answer.

'No', he said. 'BDS has been a good employer to me'.

'And you are not a member of the Union?'

'No, sir. The company deemed it inappropriate for Security staff to be in the Union'.

'So, you are not here in the interests of the Applicants or the Respondents?'

'No, sir. I am here because you asked me for an account of the incident at the gate on the day the strike started'.

I nodded again. 'I believe that, after that incident, you made an entry in the Occurrence Book which you keep at the gate, yes?'

'I did. Yes, sir'.

I passed him the photocopy which Con had supplied. 'And is that a true copy of the entry which you made?'

He scanned it. 'Yes, sir. It is'.

'And is it a true record of what took place?'

'So far as it goes, yes, sir'.

Maddox and Bailey had been whispering urgently and now Maddox was on his feet.

'I must object!' he exclaimed. 'If this document is what the witness has said it is, then it is a copy of a confidential company record, and all of BDS' internal documents are covered by the Official Secrets Act'.

The chairman turned to me. 'Is that your understanding, Mr Tyroll?'

'The document is a copy of one passed to me by another witness', I said. 'Insofar as it originates within the Respondent company, it is their property. It is not marked as classified under the Official Secrets Act, but I admit that it may be. I am quite happy to withdraw it and ask Mr Maddox to produce the original'.

Maddox rose, shaking his head. 'No, sir!' he declared. 'This copy has been illegally acquired from the company's premises. I object most strongly to its admission and I will not produce the original'.

'Is it vital to your case, Mr Tyroll?' asked the chairman. 'It is, after all, a written record made by the witness. Surely you can ask him to tell us about the events described?'

I nodded, smiling inwardly. 'I shall try to carry on without it', I said, knowing that I had got right round the problem of George Barlow not recording that his boss was drunk and I had shown the Tribunal that BDS were scared of the Tribunal seeing that entry.

I took the paper back from George and pressed on. 'On the day of the strike you were on duty at the main gate of the BDS works in Russell Road, Belston?'

'Yes, sir'.

'And throughout the morning various parties of strikers left the premises. I am not concerned with them. After the shift had arrived, did anyone come in?'

'Yes, sir. Mr Mulvaney and Mr Martin came to the gate once or twice'.

'And you admitted them?'

'Yes, sir. After I'd asked them their business on the site'.

'And what did they tell you?'

'Mr Mulvaney said that the company had alleged sabotage in previous strikes, and he wasn't going to have it said about his strike, so he wanted to make sure that each section stood down properly, leaving all work finished'.

I could have done without the 'his strike', but I passed over it, quickly. 'And you thought that was a suitable reason to admit them?'

'Yes, sir. It seemed to me that it was what the company would want'.

'Then you had a telephone call from the front office?'

'Yes, sir. It was Mr Cantrell, saying that Mr Bailey didn't want to admit Mr Mulvaney and Mr Martin again'.

'What did you do?'

'I tried to explain why I had let them in, but he said that they were probably lying about their reasons, that they were dangerous and they should not be admitted again'.

'And I believe that they arrived shortly after that call?'

'Yes, sir, and I told them that I was sorry, that I had orders not to let them in again'.

I nodded. 'And where did this conversation take place?'

'At the gate, sir.'

'They were inside the fence?'

'Well, yes, sir. They came to my office door, which is about a yard inside the wire'.

'So you were standing talking to them,

about a yard inside the wire. What happened next?'

'Someone opened a window on the main admin building. That's only about fifty yards from the gate, across to the right. Someone opened one of the ground floor windows and I could see Mr Bailey at the window, waving and shouting'.

'Could you hear what he was shouting?'

'No, sir. It wasn't the distance, but he seemed incoherent, sir. I thought he was shouting at me to send them away, so I told them again that they couldn't come in'.

'And they showed no sign of hostility at being refused entrance?'

'None that I saw, sir. In fact, Jimmy Martin laughed. They had just turned to go when Mr Bailey and Mr Cantrell and Mr Cheetham came running from the admin block'.

'And what happened?'

'Mr Bailey was in front. He was very red in the face. He came up to us and he started shouting at Mr Mulvaney.'

'Do you recall what he said?'

'I recall that it was abusive, sir. I believe the word "scum" was used'.

'By Mr Bailey?'

'Yes, sir'.

'Mr Bailey was very angry, I gather?'

'He was raging, sir. I didn't think it very good for the Management to be having a shouting match with shop stewards at the main gate, and I tried to calm him, but he shoved me aside. Then he hit Mr Mulvaney in the face'.

'He hit Mr Mulvaney in the face', I repeated. 'Was that in response to something Mr Mulvaney had said or done?'

'No, sir. He was shouting at Mr Mulvaney and then he just lashed out at him'.

'Then what happened?'

'Well, Mr Mulvaney staggered back against the side of my door, and hit out at Mr Bailey, striking him under the left eye'.

'And what did you do?'

'I moved in to stop it. Me and Mr Martin grabbed Mr Bailey and the others helped us'.

'Did Mr Martin strike a blow at Mr Bailey?'

'No, sir. He was helping us restrain Mr Bailey'.

'Were any more blows struck—by anyone?'

'No, sir. Mr Cantrell and Mr Cheetham took Mr Bailey away and Mr Martin and Mr Mulvaney went'.

'That was the end of the incident?'

'Yes, sir'.

'You have told us', I summed up, 'that Mr Bailey ran to the gate, very red-faced and extremely angry, that he abused Mr Mulvaney, calling him "scum" and that he struck him without provocation or reason, that Mr Mulvaney struck one blow in self-defence and Mr Martin struck no blows, but assisted you in restraining Mr Bailey. Did you believe that Mr

Bailey would strike again?'

'I don't know, sir, but it seemed likely and I wanted to prevent any further violence'.

'When the Applicants came to the gate, each time, do you know where they came from?'

'Yes, sir. The cafe across the street'.

'A cafe—not a public house? And were they sober on each occasion?'

'Oh, yes. sir. They were sober so far as I could see'.

'You stood and talked to them. Was there alcohol on their breath?'

'No, sir. I'd have smelt it if there was and I wouldn't have admitted them'.

'Was there alcohol on anyone's breath that day?'

He paused and shot a thoughtful glance at Bailey. 'Yes, sir, there was. When Mr Bailey was abusing Mr Mulvaney I could smell drink on his breath, and when I took hold of him it was even stronger'.

Bailey snorted and a stage whisper of 'What a surprise!' came from the rear. The chairman snapped his pencil banging for silence.

'You're a former police officer, Mr Barlow. I take it you've handled a good few drunks in your time?'

A smile flickered. 'Yes, sir. More than a few'.

'In your experienced opinion, then—was Mr Bailey drunk when he came to the gate?'

'Yes, sir', he replied, firmly

'Thank you, Mr Barlow', and I sat down.

CHAPTER THIRTY-FIVE

Maddox rose, with Bailey still whispering at him, urgently. What followed was pathetic. There is no one more difficult to cross-examine than an experienced police officer, particularly one who happens to be telling the truth.

George Barlow blocked or foiled every attempt to suggest that he was mistaken, and Maddox was reduced at last to suggesting that the witness was lying. I let this go on a little while, then intervened.

'Mr Chairman', I said as I rose, 'My friend is, I suspect, harassing this witness. He has no other line of cross-examination than the witness' honesty. Now, Mr Bailey, in his evidence, was good enough to state his belief in Mr Barlow's honesty and reliability. If Mr Maddox will concede that Mr Bailey was not telling the truth, then I will not object to his attacks on Mr Barlow's honesty'.

'Don't be flippant, Mr Tyroll', the chairman reproved me. 'At the same time, Mr Maddox, the Tribunal would prefer your cross-examination to move onto substantive matters. We have heard the witness deny that he is lying several times'.

Maddox looked helplessly at Bailey, then rose.

'There are no more matters I wish to raise with this witness, sir'.

The chairman adjourned for lunch. Con and Jimmy and their fans swarmed around George, slapping his back and shaking his hand as they pressed out into the corridor.

Sheila and I followed them, and I managed to get a word with George, to thank him. 'That must have been difficult', I said. 'I hope it hasn't got you into trouble'.

He grinned. 'Not much', he said. 'Cantrell's just told me that I retire tomorrow'.

'Cantrell?' I said, 'Is he here?'

'He's down there with the bosses', and he pointed along the corridor.

I followed his pointing finger, then turned back. I had recognised the man who was in conversation with Bailey and Maddox. 'That's not Cantrell', I began, 'that's a freelance journalist . . .' I stopped. That's a man who *told* me he was a freelance journalist called Walters, I thought.

I dived into one of the conference rooms and snatched a telephone, calling John Parry to tell him that I'd located Walters. Luckily, I got straight through to him.

'Where is he now?' was all he wanted to know.

'He's leaving the Employment Tribunal building with Bailey and Maddox from BDS. I imagine they'll be lunching together'.

'Are you sitting after lunch?'

'Yes', I said, 'but I don't know if he'll be here'.

'We'll get onto West Mid Police and get their blokes to look around. If not I'll see you at the Tribunal after lunch'.

When I got back into the corridor I saw Bailey's back disappearing into the lift. Sheila confirmed that Maddox and Walters had gone with him.

'Shall we follow them?' she suggested.

'Not likely', I said. 'I'm for lunch. The Police can do the dangerous stuff'.

Over lunch in a cafe we pushed it around again. Walters killing Samson had never made any sense, but Walters being Cantrell killing Samson made even less sense. We ended up no wiser than we started and made our way back to the Tribunal for the afternoon session.

As we came out of the lift I saw Walters/Cantrell again, still in company with Bailey and Maddox, emerging from the second lift further along the corridor. As I watched them, John Parry came up behind me.

'I've got a couple of Brummy blokes with me', he said. 'Is Cantrell here?'

I pointed along the corridor. 'That's him', I said. 'The tall bloke with short hair and a brown jacket'.

'You sure?' he asked.

'Absolutely', I said.

He turned to his two companions. 'Right', he said. 'He's your arrest. Go for it!'

I watched as they moved swiftly along the corridor. Cantrell had his back to them as they approached him. One of them tapped him on the shoulder and I heard the detective say, 'Mr Cantrell? I am Detective Sergeant Rowden and this is Detective Constable Archer. I am arresting you for the murder of . . .'

He got no further. Cantrell had swung around at the detective's touch, but as soon as he knew what they wanted he plunged straight between them and dived along the corridor.

John Parry was standing just in front of me and moved to block Cantrell reaching the stairhead, but another factor intervened.

As Cantrell dived along the corridor towards the stairs, Sheila stepped out of the Ladies', straight into his path. I'll give him credit for the fact that he hardly paused, but just took immediate advantage of the situation, scooping an arm around her and dragging her with him to the stair top.

As he reached the stairs I had every expectation that my feisty fiancée would recover from her surprise and give him a seriously hard time, but he produced a small pistol from his pocket and jammed it against her jaw as he held her.

The sight of the weapon turned everything to slow motion. Cantrell had reached the stairhead and was beginning to back slowly down the steps, grasping Sheila tightly in front of him and keeping his gun pressed against her neck. The coppers had stopped moving and members of the public were drawing away from the centre of the action.

John Parry began a slow advance to the stairhead. I stepped quickly back towards the lift which had brought us up. Once inside it, I went down to the floor below and tumbled out into an empty corridor.

I ran to the foot of the stairs and kicked off my shoes. The steps bent into two flights between this floor and the next above. To my right and above me, I could just see Cantrell's feet on the steps. I knew enough of Sheila's capabilities to know that if Cantrell lost his advantage for a split second, she would take advantage of it, and I intended to give her that chance.

Grasping the banister, I sprang silently up the stairs. It almost worked. I had just reached the landing between the two flights when Cantrell sensed my presence. At that point he was about four steps down from the top, holding Sheila above him, and the Police officers were bunched helplessly at the top of the stairs.

As he sensed, heard or saw me, he swung his head towards me. A moment later he shifted the pistol and pointed it at me.

The irrelevant thought flitted through my mind that his gun was smaller than the last one that had been pointed at me, before my mind grappled with our situation.

Cantrell could not get up the stairs. His only way out was down. I was determined that whatever happened he was not going to get past the middle landing. He had only one alternative. If he shot Sheila, or abandoned her, he would be overwhelmed by coppers from above. He had to clear his way down. That's what he tried to do. Even at the distance of a few feet between us, I saw the flash of his pistol, and felt the impact of the bullet in my left arm before I heard the shot.

There was no immediate pain, but the impact flung me back against the banister. He fired twice more, and one of the shots found a place in my left side, pulling me away from the banister. I clutched it to keep from falling.

It had worked. To fire at me, Cantrell had been forced to pull Sheila around to his side and take his attention away from her. She had not lost the opportunity. As he lined up a fourth shot, she smashed her elbow into the side of his head and grabbed his gun arm, forcing it upwards with both of her arms.

I was still standing—just—held up by my grip on the banister and a determination that Cantrell would not get past me, though I suspect that the most I could do to stop him was flop on him.

The struggle for the gun ended as it slipped from Cantrell's fingers and bounced down the stairs. He loosened his hold on Sheila and dived for the weapon. A fatal mistake. She kicked him expertly between the legs as he broke away from her. He shouted an oath and pitched forward, stumbling down the steps and falling right into me.

I couldn't even flop on him, but I didn't need to. As he staggered into me, I lost my hold on the banister and fell against the outside wall of the landing. A bright rainbow wave of pain burst in my head as I collapsed underneath him and blacked out.

CHAPTER THIRTY-SIX

The next time I saw daylight it was from a hospital bed. As I forced my eyes open, I was cheered to see Sheila's eyes staring into mine, though her freckles were standing out from her pale face as they only did when she was worried.

'Hello', I croaked.

She said nothing, but fed me some fruit juice until my mouth and tongue worked.

'You're back', she said at last.

'Are you OK?' I asked.

'I'm OK', she said, 'but what about you?'

'What about me? What's the damage?' I went to raise myself a little on an elbow and realised that it hurt, so I stayed still.

'You've got a broken upper left arm and the other bullet ran round your left ribs. It ploughed a nasty tunnel round your side, but it didn't hit anything essential. They say you'll be right'.

A young doctor stepped into the room. 'Couldn't have put it better myself', he remarked, 'only longer'.

He sat on the end of the bed. 'Well, Mr Tyroll, things don't look too bad. As Miss McKenna said, Birmingham Accident picked the scrap metal out of you and patched the holes. They didn't seem to think that deliberate shooting qualified as accident, so they shoved you back to Belston. Once we've sorted out your left arm, you'll be right in no time. The left side is going to be a nuisance. You'll need to lie down till that heals. Walking or moving will just aggravate it, but you're moderately healthy, so I don't foresee any problems', and he stood up and ambled out.

'What happened to Walters—Cantrell?' I asked.

'That bastard', she said, 'is in custody with very sore balls. West Midlands handed him over to John's lot and John reckons they've got him for the murder'.

'You didn't need to kick him so hard', I said.

'Too right, I didn't, but I'd just seen him shooting you so I wanted to mark my disapproval'.

'Sometimes I realise what it is that makes

me love you', I said.

'Yair? Well, try to show it by not getting killed, will you?'

'Does John know why Samson was killed?' I asked, changing the subject.

'Nobody knows and Cantrell ain't telling, but John reckons they've got a case anyway'.

'You surprise me', I said. Then, 'You look worn out'.

'I have been here since yesterday', she said, 'wondering why you keep on trying to get killed'.

'There's gratitude. That swine Cantrell was going to need to get rid of you once he got down the stairs. I had to stop him. Besides—I owed you a couple'.

She smiled and her eyes moistened. 'Just don't do it again, you galah!' she commanded. 'Hey, look!' she said, to distract me from her tears, 'Look at all the fan mail you've got!'

I looked at the cards and flowers on the bedside cabinet. 'How long have I been here?'

'Only since last night. Like the Doc said, they operated in Brum yesterday then shipped you back here. Look, who's this Mrs Johnstone who's sent you a card?'

I groaned. 'She's a sweet old lady whose missing husband I am supposed to find. Who else?'

'Well, there's the office, of course. There's Doc Macintyre, John Parry, Kath McBride, Tom Wellington . . .'

A tap at the door brought John Parry. 'Name the devil!' he exclaimed. 'They tell me you're sitting up and taking notice'.

'They lied', I said. 'I'm lying down in pain, trying to take notice. Sheila says you've got Mr Cantrell'.

'Oh, indeed, boyo'.

'Can you make a case for the Samson killing?'

'Well, he won't say a word, but we've got metallurgical comparisons of the rust fragments the car left at the roadside, we've got witnesses from the White Lion who've ID'd him and we've got a wonderful piece of luck'.

'What's that?'

'Samson was wearing a tweed jacket. Cantrell hit him so hard that the pattern of the tweed is impressed in the enamel of one wing. Put a low light across it and you can get a pin sharp photo of the weave. Rare but lovely!'

'If you've got the car. Have you?'

'Oh yes. West Mercia found it for us, stashed in a shed on his boss' farm in Shropshire'.

'Who's his boss?'

'Dennis Maiden'.

'Dennis Maiden!' I exclaimed, and winced. 'The man who took the ponies. Cantrell works for him?'

'Yep. Cantrell ran MSA—Midland Security Agency'.

'Then that', I said, 'connects him with Samson. Samson said that Maiden's Security Manager was awkward about giving the ponies back. So they had met, at least once'.

John nodded. 'Even we dim plods have managed to work that out, but it doesn't provide a motive'.

My mind was surging back to activity, trying to piece patterns together out of odds and ends.

'So Cantrell and Samson meet over the ponies', I began, falteringly. 'Then Cantrell goes to the Tribunal, pretending to be a journalist—why?'

'So no one would know who he was', said John.

'But the BDS blokes would have known. They must have seen their new Security Manager'.

'Yair', said Sheila, 'but they wouldn't know that unmarked table at the back was only for the press. They wouldn't think it odd he was there'.

'But why was he there?' I demanded.

'Because he wanted to keep an eye on things, I suppose', said Sheila.

'But he stopped, after the first lunchtime', I protested.

'After he saw you with Samson', said John. 'Then he went off, sussed out Samson's movements, confirmed them with the meeting in the pub and saw him off the next night.

After which he stayed away from the Tribunal. If your witness hadn't told you who he really was, you wouldn't have known'.

'It doesn't make sense!' I protested.

'Oh yes, it does', said Sheila and John nodded. I stared at them.

'It makes sense', said Sheila, 'if it was you he was avoiding, if it was you who mustn't know he worked for BDS'.

'But I've never seen him before in my life till the Tribunal sat. Then I thought he was a reporter'.

'It only makes sense', said John, 'if he thought that Samson might somehow identify him to you. That must be why he killed him'.

I shook my head and winced again. 'But I don't know why!'

'Well, boyo, you'd better lie there and think about it, because I'm going to come and ask you officially'.

The door swung open and the space was filled by a large, black nurse.

'Mr Tyroll!' she declaimed, 'You are supposed to be recovering from gunshot wounds, surgery and anaesthesia! You, Detective Inspector, can go about your business, and you, Miss McKenna, can go home to bed and leave Mr Tyroll to me!'

They fled without argument, leaving me to Nurse Elphinstone's robust attentions and to fall asleep in a puzzled whirl.

CHAPTER THIRTY-SEVEN

I stayed puzzled. God knows, I had plenty of time to turn it all over while I recuperated, but none of the pieces would stay in place. What earthly harm could Cantrell have feared from me? None. I never knew the bloke. John Parry came back and asked me officially and I still couldn't help him.

The long hospital days passed. Visitors came and went. The Tribunal, which had adjourned hastily after the shooting, set a new date, which I could not attend, so my assistant, Alasdair, stood in for me. Working from Sheila's notes and mine and with Sheila at his side, he made the closing argument for the Applicants. The Tribunal reserved its judgement. An ominous sign. That usually means that they're trying to think of reasons to chuck the application out.

When the hospital finally chucked me out, Sheila laid on a celebration dinner. Alasdair was there and John Parry, Doc Macintyre and Claude the Phantom, our enquiry agent.

Once the food was done and the whisky circulating, Alasdair drew an envelope from his pocket.

'I have news!' he announced. 'I have here the Tribunal's decision!'

I groaned. 'Why spoil the party?'

He raised a hand. 'Listen to the opening'. He unfolded the papers and read:

'"We think it only right that, before setting out our decisions in this matter, we express our regret that Mr Tyroll, who represented the Applicants throughout the hearing, was unable to finish the case, and it is the opinion of all of us that his actions in defending the public and preventing the escape of an armed criminal deserve the highest praise—" What about that, Chris?'

'That's you, McKenna—the public', Parry muttered.

'I'm deeply touched', I said, 'now go on to the bit where they throw us out'.

Alasdair smiled and closed the sheaf of papers. 'Without boring the company with all the details, the fact is that they found for the Applicants. Mohammed Afsar was wrongly dismissed in breach of the Agreement, Jimmy Martin was not a cause of the strike, and there was no assault at the gate'.

'But what about the illegal strike?' I asked, amazed.

'Ah! Well, they do suggest that the strike was probably illegal, but they took your point about the Human Rights Act. They thought Bailey had ignored both the Agreement and the Act and that the dismissals were unlawful. Reinstatements at BDS they thought would be unworkable, so compensation is to be worked out between the parties'.

Applause ran round the table. Somebody called, 'Speech! Speech!'

I rapped for silence with a knife. 'Unaccustomed as I am to winning cases in the Employment Tribunals, I can only say that I am overwhelmed. It's all too good to be true!'

'It gets better', said Alasdair. 'You remember Mrs Johnstone?'

'The lady who was worried that her absent husband hadn't divorced her, yes'.

'Well, I made a few enquiries in Scotland, and back came a letter. Mr Johnstone didn't divorce her, but he died without making a will, so she's inherited a house in Aberdeen plus his savings'.

Another round of laughter and applause.

'All we need now', said John Parry, 'is a real legal success, like explaining why Cantrell murdered Samson. At the moment, the Crown Prosecution Service are saying we've a better chance of doing him for the attempted murder of Christopher Tyroll, and it goes against the grain, sending people down for trying to murder solicitors'.

Sheila smiled. 'Do you really want to know what it was all about, John?'

'Well, it would be nice, yes. Tidy, like'.

She reached for her handbag on the sideboard and pulled out a packet of photographs.

'While Chris has been lying at death's door...'

'Even a lawyer ought to give up lying there', muttered John.

'As I was saying', she continued, firmly, 'While Chris was recovering from serious injuries inflicted when an armed criminal escaped from three detectives and held a helpless female hostage, I have been answering the many fan letters he has had. One of them was from poor Kath McBride. When I went to answer hers, I remembered that Sylvie Wellington had given me some photos of Sean at a party just before he died'.

She slid the pictures out onto the table.

'These', she said, 'were taken at the engagement party of one of Sylvie's friends. Look at the date on them'.

She held one up and everybody craned to look at it. I leaned over and looked at one of the pictures on the table. It was date-marked, 14.05,12th May. I didn't see the point.

Sheila selected three pictures and laid them in a row. 'This one', she said, pointing to the right-hand end, 'is the car park of the pub and some of Sylvie's friends. The door to the pub's lounge bar is on the right rear and Sean is near the left. These other two are after the photographer gave the camera to Scan. He's not in either group, so he's probably taking the piccys'.

'The middle one is just the engagement party skylarking on the car park. This one', and she pointed to the left-hand end one, 'is the same group, but looking further left, so that you can see another door of the pub. You can even read the sign above the door. It says, "Private Dining Room", and there's a couple of blokes coming out of the door, but they're turning their heads back and you can't see their faces'.

She reached into her handbag again and pulled out a larger picture, then laid another photograph on the table. 'This one', she said, 'is still looking to the left, and this time the blokes coming out of the Dining Room have walked right out onto the car park and the camera has caught them. I had that one enlarged'.

She laid the larger picture down and we all craned.

'I wondered', Sheila said, 'why I thought I recognised Goatly when he gave evidence. There he is—him and Cantrell and Bailey, having a private get-together two nights before Mohammed Afsar was sacked. What do you think that means, John?'

'Who's Goatly?' he said.

'Goatly', I explained, 'is the Union's Midland Secretary, who backed the company's action so far that he came along to give evidence for them. Con Mulvaney got me a copy of Goatly's report to the National Secretary. It was word-for-word the same as the fax that BDS sent their Coventry works to stop the strike spreading'.

John picked up the picture and looked at it. 'That's certainly Cantrell, and you say the other two are Goatly and who?'

'Bailey—the Managing Director of BDS', I said. 'What we've got here is a collusive strike, provoked by management for its own purposes'.

'What purposes, though?' wondered John.

'Easy', Alasdair chimed in. 'Finance. Provoking a strike is an old management trick for easing a cash flow problem. You get rid of the larger part of your payroll for as long as you want. According to the evidence, the arguments at BDS were always about undermanning. Well, you don't do that unless you've got cash flow problems. BDS was in a squeeze, hoping for Retaliator to come up trumps and the Americans to sign up'.

'But how would a strike help them?' Macintyre asked. 'It only delays things'.

'Things were already delayed', said Sheila. 'Something was going wrong at Coventry and Belston was having to sit on its hands and wait for Coventry. A strike at Belston saved BDS money, gave Coventry time to get their act in order and gave BDS an excuse for delays other than Coventry's incompetence'.

'The Yanks don't like strikes', Claude commented.

'So they don't,' I said, 'but Bailey could show them a tough face. He sacked the trouble-makers right away, and as soon as a strike started at Coventry he had Goatly's help to squash it'.

'Which is all very tidy, as a lefty theory of capitalist wickedness and all that', said John, 'but how does it bear on Cantrell killing Samson?'

'It bears', said Sheila, 'on Cantrell killing Sean McBride, Charlie Nesbit and Samson'.

We all looked at her, openmouthed.

'That's what the piccys are!' she snapped. 'The reason'.

We were still slow on the uptake so she went on.

'On May 12th, Cantrell, Bailey and Goatly met to make or finalise their plan. Coming out of the pub they walked into the flash of a camera wielded by Sean McBride. We know Cantrell's a sensitive soul. He wasn't going to have a damning photo like that lying about, so he tracked Sean down and, just like he did with Samson, he sussed out his movements. Only that time he paid Charlie Nesbit for the information'.

'But why did he need to kill Sean?' Claude enquired.

'Because he'd already turned over his kip and not found the photos. He found out about the garage from Charlie, went there and offed Sean quite simply by sliding that piece back into place on the roof. Perhaps he just meant to knock Sean out so he could search the garage. When he couldn't find the pictures there, he gave up. Then Charlie started his sad little tricks with the tape and it got in the papers, so he saw Charlie off, as well'.

'So what was all that wi' the song on the phone?' asked Mac.

'Charlie can't have failed to realise that the bloke who paid him was the cause of Sean's death, but he couldn't have understood why. He thought that Sylvia was next in line. In his own peculiar way he was trying to tell someone that there was going to be a second death. Never thought it would be his, I suppose'.

'I still don't see the connection with Samson', John said.

'The connection', she said, 'is sitting right here—Mr Christopher Tyroll. Cantrell knew Chris was in the BDS case, he must have known he was involved with Sean's case. He didn't want Chris putting the two together. When he saw Samson and Chris talking, he had to knock out Samson in case he let the cat out of the bag'.

'Pretty ruthless!' Claude remarked.

'The profits of BDS were at stake', I said. 'I wonder what the Americans are paying for Retaliator'.

'I wonder what Bailey was paying Cantrell to set things up for him—and Goatly'.

'And there would almost certainly have been a large chunk of personal profit', said Alasdair. 'There were stories about selling short on the BDS strike'.

'What's "selling short"?' asked John. 'We poor plods don't have much chance to speculate in stocks'.

'If you have confidential information that a firm is going to find itself in trouble', explained Alasdair, 'you offer to sell lots of shares in it which you haven't got. Then the trouble happens, people start dumping their shares in the firm, and you buy them up cheap and fill the orders to sell'.

'Why would you do that?' asked John.

'Because you sell at the high price agreed before the trouble, but you buy at the low price when the trouble has made the shares slump. I'll bet Bailey, Maiden, even Goatly and Cantrell, have made a mint out of knowing in advance that BDS would be hit by a strike'.

John finished his drink and rose. 'I hate to drink and run', he said, 'but I think I've got phone calls to make', and he left, taking the photos with him.

So it all turned out better than I expected for Mohammed and Con and Jimmy. It turned out worse for Bailey, who was chucked out as MD as soon as he had been arrested, and Goatly, who took early retirement from the Union. Sniffing around their share dealings produced a lot of suspicion but no hard evidence. Cantrell got life for two murders, so they didn't bother with poor Samson or with me. In the end the losers were Samson and his family, Charlie Nesbit, Sean McBride and his family and Sylvia Wellington who would never forget Sean.

All because a few people were hypnotised by profit and a Coroner didn't want public embarrassment in his Court.

Sheila, of course, had a different slant on it. 'You know', she said, once we were in bed, 'watching the English legal system at work is an experience of great value to a social historian. It's like watching the nineteenth century come alive'.

'Huh!' I said. 'In the nineteenth century trade unionists didn't get to appear before Employment Tribunals. They got to appear at Assizes, who shipped them off to some unbelievably barbaric colony in the Pacific'.

'Shut up and make love to me!' she commanded. 'It's been ages'.

'I'm a sick man. I've got a bad arm'.

'Who needs arms?' she asked, and proved her point.

We hope you have enjoyed this Large Print book. Other Chivers Press or Thorndike Press Large Print books are available at your library or directly from the publishers.

For more information about current and forthcoming titles, please call or write, without obligation, to:

Chivers Large Print
published by BBC Audiobooks Ltd
St James House, The Square
Lower Bristol Road
Bath BA2 3SB
UK
email: bbcaudiobooks@bbc.co.uk
www.bbcaudiobooks.co.uk

OR

Thorndike Press
295 Kennedy Memorial Drive
Waterville
Maine 04901
USA
www.gale.com/thorndike
www.gale.com/wheeler

All our Large Print titles are designed for easy reading, and all our books are made to last.

SC
white 5/14

mysteries of Laura